EVIL SEED

Book 3

Robbie Kesselring

Copyright 2026 by Robbie Kesselring

ISBN: 978-1-969422-73-7 (Paperback)
       978-1-969422-74-4 (Ebook)

All rights reserved. No part of this book may be reproduced, distributed or transmitted in any form or by any means, including photocopying, recording or other electronic or mechanical methods, without the prior written permission of the publisher, except in the case of brief quotations embodied in critical reviews and other noncommercial uses permitted by copyright law.

The views expressed in this book are solely those of the author and do not necessarily reflect the views of the publisher, and the publisher hereby disclaims any responsibility of them.

Olympus Story House
www.olympusstoryhouse.com

TABLE OF CONTENTS

Prologue

There is new life on the City in Space, Purgatory. And not just one, but two. One carries the chromosomes of an antediluvian nemesis. The other possesses genetics of an enhanced man, myself, gifted to me by a Messenger. What will my wife think? She's barely had a chance to get used to me. Even a physically intimate relationship is new to her. Now she's pregnant! Like most of everything else in her life on the City in Space, another new experience. Will this one be as welcome as the others?

We've never talked about children or having babies. Neko has always been career-minded, a workaholic. Having a baby will certainly alter her lifestyle, hopefully in a pleasing way.

I'll muster up the courage to tell her myself.

Resnik thought further.

What about Hera Wombosie? She also needs to know. Hera is pregnant as well.

It won't be easy for her to accept. The creature that mated her did so while she was under his trance. As of yet, Hera isn't aware she was violated. It won't be easy for her to hear. Our city counselor, Summer Genosis, will accompany me to enlighten Hera and offer support. My ability to heal should also be a sanative relief to any unwelcome vehement emotions.

Kids

The first day of school found two five-year-old boys showing up early. The principal, Kassi Pagoni, was waiting for them. The two new students appear to be a balance of opposites. Neko's son, Gettie, has milky white skin and bright gray eyes, topped with pitch-black hair. He is over average height for his age. Hera's son, Raf (Rafykei), is even taller. He has midnight-colored skin contrasted with white hair. His eyes look like two black holes in space. It's quite a juxtaposition when the boys are seen together, which is more common than not. They became best friends almost from birth. To that point in time, they were the first babies born off-planet on the City in Space, Purgatory, which has since experienced several additional births over the past five years.

The city administrator, Resnik Clayborn, released the two small hands he was holding. Kassi then took over that task in order to take the boys to their first class. Being a small woman, her hands are just slightly bigger than that of the two larger-than-average kindergartners.

"You guys be good today," said Resnik. "I love you." His eyes connected with both boys.

"I love you, Dad," said Gettie.

"I love you, sir," said Raf.

Resnik had become a father to both boys. Raf's mother, Hera, was totally on board with Resnik becoming a surrogate dad to her son. There was no man she respected more. There was actually no man she liked more—even loved more. In Hera's heart, she was still in love with Resnik, though after those feelings caused big problems in the past, Hera decided to forever keep a lid on her unrequited affections.

The boys sat next to each other in the unfamiliar classroom. The open-air style of the school offered a welcoming aura for all new students. Gettie and Raf liked most things as long as they were experiencing them together. This latest adventure suited them fine. The biggest challenge would be keeping the boys focused. Students were allowed to stand by their desks during a typical school day, which helped the fidgety children. However, having no glass in the window openings was invoking quite a distraction for the two five-year-olds. They were used to having the freedom to explore all of the 1.5 mile cube of Purgatory. Resnik deemed it the safest city anywhere.

One day found Gettie and Raf in the pond used to breed sashimi fish. They were caught "neck deep" along the shoreline. When confronted, the soaked boys said, "We were just trying to catch dinner."

This kind of behavior was typical for the young boys. They were the epitome of larking.

Both of them seemed to be equally matched with physical strength and a curious nature. Raf was always taller than Gettie and a bit more aggressive. He would occasionally lead Gettie into situations his best friend wouldn't normally be interested in, like climbing the Kitayama cedar tree. Resnik had told the boys to leave it alone. It was the tallest tree in the Garden of Neom, which was located next to Purgatory. Its multiple spires of *daisugi*-trimmed trunks looked very enticing to both boys. The trunks were immature, yet tall and narrow. A few were close to each other, close enough to make the climb more manageable.

The temptation for Raf to ascend overwhelmed him. Gettie followed. The misadventure ended with splinters and scratches from the bark, as well as being grounded and extra chores for the two young explorers.

Later that night, Resnik had a talk with his son. "You've got to stop letting Raf talk you into stuff."

"He made it sound so fun, Dad," pleaded Gettie.

"Fun doesn't mean it's okay to do it. You need to be a better leader to Raf. It will keep both of you out of trouble—or at least, less trouble."

Gettie's young mind seemed to grasp what his dad said. He decided from that time forward to be a more responsible friend to Raf.

Progression

The City in Space had grown in the past six years. Purgatory benefited greatly by the absence of Dark Matter, the interstellar nemesis of mankind's establishment in space. The shadow beasts of Dark Matter had been contained on the planet TrES-2b. Resnik and his crew fought through hell in order to contain the remainder of the Legion of Dark Dragons to their home, the Dark Planet. Purgatory and its people have since enjoyed freedom from the prideful-controlling influence of Dark Matter. The shadow beasts had taken three of the city's citizens by manipulating their minds through dark emotions, the chief of which was pride. Hera was one of these; Othneal and Rumi were the other two.

Rumi died on the Dark Planet (TrES-2b) while helping Resnik and his crew. Othneal was rescued along with Hera.

With the containment of Dark Matter, all focus has now been back on the advancement of Purgatory and its connected facility, Neom.

Neom is a round garden dome 1.5 miles in diameter. The garden is designed to grow plants and animals in order to sustain the population of the City in Space. With the help of Hera (the farm director) and Yasti, the entomologist, Neom has thrived. Yasti is also a member of the crew that travels into space with Resnik. She was tasked to watch over Resnik by a divine entity called the Messenger. This same type of being bestowed special abilities upon Resnik ten years previously in order to aid the establishing and continuation of Purgatory. Now six years after her arrival on Purgatory, she spends most of her time concerned with Neom's pollinating insects.

Traveling through space in Guardian tubes has become more about recreation and exploration rather than searching for destructive creatures, although the crew still occasionally enters a tube (formerly known as wormholes) in order to receive technology from a Guardian. A Guardian dwells on every planet, moon, or star. They transfer tech information directly to Resnik's mind so he can apply it for the advancement of Purgatory and Neom. The individuals in charge of utilizing this technology are all brilliant themselves. Most live on the city. Others visit periodically. Makan Pied is one that occasionally makes the journey to the City in Space. His contribution to Purgatory is water. It's also Makan's passion. He's been working on establishing rain clouds in an enclosed environment. The Garden of Neom is his current focus.

To date, clouds have formed within the great dome of Neom. They have released mist and fog; however, there is still no outright rain.

Pure, recycled water in Purgatory is cleaner than rainwater on Earth thanks to Makan. Many citizens on the City in Space can no longer live on their polluted home planet. Both water and air on Earth have become compromised. Also, the atmosphere on Earth has become saturated with communication signals of all kinds. Radio waves and powerful microwave transmissions are affecting the well-being of people all over the planet. It seems everyone worldwide has a cell phone.

Purgatory has become renowned for the ultimate healthy lifestyle. Trust in the safety of a City in Space is gaining the confidence of many grounded on Earth. The need to make room for more citizens is of paramount concern for Resnik. The obvious choice is to expand upward. The cube shape of Purgatory could allow many layers of housing for people migrating from Earth.

It's time to have a talk with Neko, thought Resnik.

She had been the original city designer for Purgatory. Neko was currently splitting her time between Earth and the City in

Space. Al- Ula, Saudi Arabia, has become her second home. A horse named Kurokaze is her favorite pastime. Resnik had shown her the basics of horsemanship, and Neko extrapolated further. Her love of the horse, along with a passion for riding, manifested in the frequency of her trips to Earth. Her job working for Sheikh Khalil was really a side note. Along with her husband Resnik and son Gettie, the horse Kurokaze has filled her heart fuller than she could have ever imagined. In Neko's mind, bringing the beloved horse to the City in Space would be the best of both worlds. Unfortunately, Kurokaze was owned by the sheikh, not her. Besides, Purgatory may not be ready to accommodate such a large animal, at least not yet.

Resnik decided the time was overdue for a visit to Earth. He wanted to connect with his beloved wife Neko. Several weeks away from each other was simply too long. Plus, he wanted to share his thoughts concerning utilizing more empty space within the atmosphere of Purgatory. It is, after all, very tall and could accommodate many more people. Many on Earth have been inquiring about moving to the City in Space.

This visit to Earth will include the boys. Resnik feels occasional trips to Earth make Gettie and Raf stronger. The gravity on Earth is stronger than that of Purgatory.

The City in Space shares gravity between the moon and sun. It doesn't create its own, hence the gravitational pull is less. Humans returning to Earth from space become heavier and eventually grow stronger.

The boys love going to Earth. It's an adventure they enjoy repeating. They like hanging out with the horse Kurokaze, but what they really like is exploring Resnik's farm. After a few days of getting used to Earth's air, Earth's smells, and Earth's gravity, Gettie and Raf always hit the ground running.

The first stop, however, will be al-Ula, where Neko works. An hour and a half flight in the spacecraft *Ornan* followed by a short flight in an Earth jet brought the three of them to Sheikh Khalil's compound. Neko will be joining them soon, her office is just a short drive from the compound and the beloved horse. While waiting, Resnik took the boys to see Kurokaze. The Prince of Horses snorted in recognition of the three fellows. He stuck his head through an opening in the gate, bringing it down to the young ones. Kurokaze allowed Gettie and Raf to touch his soft nose while nostrils flared. Resnik put his hand on the horse's forehead.

"Good to see you, old friend," uttered Resnik.

His touch seemed to bring calmness to the special horse.

"Can we ride him this time, Dad?" asked Gettie.

"That's up to your mom, son."

Raf moved in closer to Kurokaze, sniffing back to the horse, sort of sharing breath with the large animal. His hand moved along the horse's powerful jaw and back to its muscular neck, which became accessible while Kurokaze was lowering his head. Raf was more anxious to ride than Gettie. He wondered what it would be like to sit on the tall horse, high above everyone.

"*Konnichiwa* [hello], boys."

A slender woman with long black hair and catlike eyes entered the barn. She was wearing her usual work clothes— loose-fitting, long- flowing beautiful garments. Gettie turned to face the barn door and ran to the open arms of his mother. With lean but strong arms, Neko hoisted her son in order to hold him close. A kiss followed.

"I think you're heavier than last time I saw you."

"I am. I get tired just walking on this planet," answered Gettie.

She understood what he meant and let his comment pass without notice. "I missed you."

She off-loaded Gettie to hug Resnik. He put one hand around her back and with the other patted her hindquarters.

Neko then turned her attention to Raf. She still found it

difficult to be affectionate to Raf. His mother had caused Neko much grief in the past. She put effort into not transferring any ill feelings she may feel about Hera upon Raf. Neko tried not to hold him responsible for his mother's misgivings. She also really appreciated the close friendship Raf held with her son Gettie. Neko kneeled down and once again opened her arms, this time making eye contact with the slightly taller boy who possessed thick white hair. His face displayed a look of relief mixed with gladness. Raf immediately approached Neko and welcomed her embrace.

"Hello, Miss Neko."

"Hello, Raf. Do you want to ride Kurokaze today?"

He managed a very charming smile.

"Yes, ma'am."

"You boys lead Kurokaze out to the big arena and let him run off some energy. I'll be right back," Neko left for the guest house to change into cowgirl clothes.

Resnik slipped a halter over Kurokaze's head and neck then gave the lead rope to the two young boys. They both grasped it and held on tight. Their efforts were overkill; the once dangerous horse has developed a very stable demeanor. So much so that Neko was planning on riding double or even triple with the boys.

Kurokaze was let loose in the arena. He did what he was bred to do, run. Head and tail went up. He behaved like a true Arabian horse. He looked beautiful while he ran effortlessly, his long black mane flowing as he strode. By the time Neko made her way into the arena, Kurokaze had tired a bit and was ready to be saddled. Neko was wearing spandex riding pants and boots. Resnik's eyes were drawn to her long legs.

"You look good, honey," he said while offering to give her a lift up in the saddle.

"Thanks, *akago* [babe]."

Once mounted, Neko asked for both boys to join her. Resnik obliged by setting Raf behind her and Gettie on the saddle in front of her.

"Okay, guys, try not to hold on with your legs. Raf, you hold on to the back of the saddle. Son, you hold the saddle horn."

It looked a little unorthodox; however, the horse seemed fine with it. He loved Neko very much and would probably do anything for her. Both boys nervously held on with eyes wide. Neko gave Kurokaze the cue to move ahead slowly by gently squeezing with her lower legs. The boys stiffened a little while trying not to grab the horse with their own legs. It was a new sensation. Riding high on a large animal suited both boys; however, feeling the horse's muscles and bones moving beneath them would take some getting used to. As was typical, Raf embraced the experience before Gettie. He liked the idea that someone can control the movements of a big, strong animal like Kurokaze. Also, being elevated while riding pleased him.

Gettie simply enjoyed doing something special with his mom. He found comfort sitting close to her as she confidently directed the horse. Neko's arms were encircling her son while holding the reins. As the three of them moved across the arena, Neko gradually increased the speed. The faster cadence made the boys giggle as they began bouncing against the horse. Once they settled down a bit, she asked the boys if they wanted to go faster. Almost simultaneously, they said yes. Off they went. Neko's hair was blowing in Raf's face. Kurokaze's thick black mane was encompassing Gettie's chest and head.

Neko lifted her son's hands in order to place the reins in them. She kept her hands on his, holding them gently but firmly. Gettie's face appeared focused and maybe a little shocked. He remained calm, leaning against his mother. After a minute or so, she slowly began to ease back on the reins. When the horse came to a stop, the woman of few words put her hands around her son for a hug and a kiss on the top of his head.

"Thanks, Mom," uttered Gettie.

"Thanks, ma'am," said Raf. He slid off the back of Kurokaze.

Gettie waited for his mom to dismount, then he followed. Neko attempted to help; he denied her effort.

"I got it, Mom." He wasn't going to let Raf outdo him.

Just then, someone entered the arena.

Clash of the Titans

A handsome dark-haired man wearing a *thawb* and *ghutra* was walking toward the riders and horse. Resnik, who was watching, also started walking in the same direction. He invoked the Arab's attention.

"Hello, Prince," said Resnik in a direct tone.

Prince Qusay stopped in his tracks. He was startled and somewhat dismayed to see Neko's husband. Qusay returned the greeting in a deep resonating voice. "Good day, Mr. Clayborn." He touched his forehead with his right hand.

Qusay was Sheikh Khalil's son and a member of the House of Princes. By paternal right, he was the owner of Kurokaze. He had come to check on the special horse and, even more so, Neko. His interest in Resnik's wife went way back. Before Gettie was born and before she was joined with Resnik, Qusay offered to give the special horse to Neko. This overture came with an undertone of her also committing to a relationship with himself. This offer would have been more than enough for most women. The prince was very handsome, with deep dark eyes and a bold nose. When he was not wearing his *ghutra*, a shock of thick black hair could be seen. However, Neko's heart already belonged to another, besides she had learned that humility far outweighed pride. And Qusay was very proud. Within seconds of his proposal, Neko exited his presence and made her way back to Purgatory. Prince Qusay wasn't used to hearing the word no or being denied much of anything. He never got over Neko's refusal. Qusay took it upon himself to eventually get the upper hand on Resnik and perhaps win the favor of Neko. His pride wouldn't allow him to let it go even after six years.

He was always on edge when around Resnik.

Today he was taken aback to find Mr. Clayborn back on Earth and in the barn. Qusay tolerated Resnik but just so. The prince didn't like Neko's husband and viewed him as a competition. Qusay had grown up with horses and resented the fact that Resnik also held knowledge of horsemanship. The prince was also feeling territorial.

This is my arena. I don't want him here! He thought.

He wished total authority had been given to him. Withal, his father is still alive and in charge of all family property. Resnik had even contributed to that fact. Sheikh Khalil developed a sickness about a year previously. Doctors were stumped as to the cure. The sheikh's life was at risk.

Resnik was able to cure him, putting Mr. Clayborn deeply in the good graces of Qusay's father.

This became yet another reason for the prince's disdain of Resnik.

Qusay had been given much from his youth until now. In fact, it may be more difficult to determine what *hadn't* been given to Prince Qusay. Now he wanted what Resnik had: favor from his father, affection from Neko, and Qusay's secret desire: control of Purgatory.

Resnik returned the prince's greeting by touching his own heart, then his mouth, finally his forehead. He knew the customs of Arabs by now. Touching his heart meant an emotional connection with the other person, such as friendship. Touching his mouth meant he would be likely to express kind words to that individual. Lastly, touching one's hand to your own forehead meant you possess pleasant thoughts toward the other person.

Resnik didn't necessarily consider Qusay a friend; he could sense animosity toward himself coming from the prince. Resnik was instead honoring Qusay's father, the sheikh. After all, Neko and Resnik were privileged guests on the compound. Allowing

Neko access to the beloved and expensive horse manifested itself into quite a favor. Treating the sheikh's son courteously would certainly weigh in Resnik and Neko's favor.

As the two titans approached each other, Resnik extended his hand to offer an American greeting. Qusay reluctantly obliged to shake hands with his rival. Resnik could instantly discern the demeanor and even the attitude of the person he was shaking hands with. Qusay's hand came in fast with a premature grasp. Resnik could feel the prince's aggression. He countered Qusay's early grab by squeezing with added force. Qusay had the advantage; he held Resnik's fingers more than his entire hand. Resnik powered through this disadvantage as he had many times in his youth. He was practically unbeatable when any arm-wrestling challenge came his way. Many opponents had also tried unorthodox grips and preempting the start of a challenge.

The simple handshake with Qusay now became a battle of strength. Qusay is slightly shorter than Resnik, and his hands are a little smaller. Resnik has the "working hands" of a carpenter. Being a little younger than Resnik, Qusay had youth on his side. It was to no avail. Resnik applied full force to Qusay's hand. The prince returned the effort in kind. His furrowed eyebrows could not hide the determined counterforce applied to Resnik's hand. Resnik's appearance remained stoic while his strength overpowered that of Qusay. The prince began relaxing his own hand in submission. The clash was over. The only consolation Qusay held in his mind was that he may have received some sort of healing from Resnik, as his father had. Qusay was present when Resnik cured his father, though he didn't want to believe Mr. Clayborn was fully responsible for that act of restoration. Qusay was also aware of other tales of the renowned "healer."

By shaking his hand, I will have gained something, thought Qusay.

The contrary was true. If anything, Prince Qusay felt a bit lesser, somehow diminished, perhaps more than just being overpowered by Resnik's strength. The disappointed prince shortened his planned visit with Neko. He quickly walked toward her while displaying a greeting, touching his heart, mouth, and forehead this time. He briefly gave his horse a few pats then exited the arena, harboring a higher level of contempt toward Resnik.

In the Forest

An earth jet followed by a multiprop electric airplane landed Resnik's family and Raf at a small-town airport. A very brief drive in an electric pickup brought the four of them across railroad tracks and down a long curvy driveway to the end of the road. A quaint farmstead surrounded by giant cottonwood trees awaited them. The boys had their anxious faces pressed against the pickup windows, anticipating the adventure that lay ahead.

"Before you guys take off, help carry in the bags," said Resnik as he glanced in the rear-view mirror. He knew the boys would want to get reacquainted with the grounds around the house and barn.

Spring was just around the corner on this secluded part of Earth. Neko exited the truck and breathed in the country air. It was so different from that of Purgatory. It was thick with smells. The trees, the river, and crop fields mixed with pollution offered a potent aroma, very much unlike the new-car scent of the City in Space.

"I'll see if there's enough food for supper. You wanna get settled in?" said Resnik.

Neko gave a slight nod. She knew her husband could make something tasty out of minimal ingredients. He went inside the charming country house to take inventory of any available food.

The cupboards were looking bare. There was just a smattering of canned goods, mostly vegetables and a small amount of canned fruit. Only condiments could be found in the fridge.

The boys came running in. "Can we go into the forest?" asked Gettie.

Raf was also looking at Resnik with anticipation.

"Aren't you guys hungry?" asked Resnik.

Both youngsters said no at the same time. Resnik knew they must be hungry but were putting their stomachs aside for the sake of exploration. He glanced at Neko; she gave him her signature nod.

"Okay, guys, let's go." He grabbed a backpack and threw in a knife, a handgun, and his Earth cell phone. It was late in the day, but plenty of light left on this midspring afternoon. The three of them left through the front door and were off toward the river that led them to adventure. The boys were focused. They were on a mission and stayed right behind Resnik while walking across varied terrain. It started with short young grass transitioning to last year's cornstalk stubble. The curve in the river was just minutes away. The smell of water began to invade their noses. It seemed like just a short time ago, Resnik and Neko had to periodically carry each boy on such a walk. This time the boys managed to dodge corn stalks while keeping up with Resnik. He wanted to take a slight detour in order to check out the pond. It had been growing in size the last couple of years. Resnik was curious to see if it was continuing to expand. Beavers had built a massive dam that blocked the large drainage tube. The pond is located just across the two sets of railroad tracks. Before the beavers created the pond, it was a marsh.

When the three of them got close, they could hear the sound of rushing water. Then the loud *beep-beep-beep* of a machine backing up. It became clear that the machine had destroyed the beaver's house, unblocking the drainage area. Several waterfowl were beginning to fly off.

The excess water flow filled up the small, normally slow-moving creek on the opposite side of the raised tracks.

"You guys wanna follow the water to the river?" asked Resnik.

They responded with an enthusiastic "Yeah!"

The three guys set off to chase the water down the winding, fast- moving stream. This was a rare opportunity. Only during a flood would the creek be so full. It was really cool to see so much liquid life in it. As they closed in on the river, the creek got narrower and the water, more concentrated. The bank on both sides is high and steep. It's really the only place to cross it, at least without walking back to the tracks. Resnik decided to attempt the crossing. There is a small tree halfway up the far side. The only way up the steep incline was to jump across and grab the roots of the tree. Resnik deemed it possible. He also thought once on the other side, he could easily get the boys over. Without much hesitation, he leaped. The root he aimed for had a second one next to and behind where Resnik was intending to grasp. He couldn't see the second from his vantage point. His fingers hit both roots but weren't able to curl around either. He slid down the steep dirt embankment incredibly fast. Before he could blink, Resnik was in the quick-moving water. The flow took his feet first. He was thrown back. The backpack became partially immersed along with his pants, shoes, and sleeves. Since the creek is so narrow at that point, Resnik was able to stabilize himself.

He tried to plant his feet into the mud on the bottom while putting a hand on both sides of the creek. He had to fight against the fast- moving water that was up to his waist. He chanced a glance to look up at two scared faces on the far bank.

"I'm okay, boys. Don't come in."

"We can help, Dad," said Gettie.

"I know, son. You guys walk back around, and if I'm not out by then, you can help. Go quickly in case I need you."

They were off in a flash.

Resnik didn't want to get carried into the river, and it was only feet away. The water was really churning at that point. He was fighting the current while stretching his arms out, putting a hand on each shore.

The contents of the pack were on his mind. It's possible they were still dry or at least mostly untouched by water. He wanted to keep it that way. Plus, being thrown into a deep river, donning water-soaked boots and clothes would be difficult, even dangerous. Resnik worked his way back to where the tree was. He was walking slowly and deliberately, planting his feet on the creek bottom, while continuing to steady himself by touching each embankment. It took everything he had to fight the fast-moving water. He extended one leg onto the shore opposite of the tree and pushed himself above the water. He then lifted his other leg out of the creek. Resnik laid his body flat on the ground so as to grab a different root. He hoisted himself up the dry ground. He then positioned his body on the upward side of the tree trunk.

Success! He thought.

However, he wasn't out of trouble yet. Even while lying against the tree, there was still more steep wall of loose earth above him. Resnik dug small indentations into the dirt with his fingers. He slipped his knees in them, then his feet. This dirt ladder allowed him to get to the top. Once there, he could hear footsteps; the boys had arrived.

"Hey, Dad," said Gettie while breathing heavily, trying to catch his breath.

"You made it, sir," said Raf. He had bloody elbows and was holding a rabbit by its hind legs.

Resnik was getting to his feet. "Whatcha got there?"
"Supper."

Gettie chimed in. "It didn't slow us down, Dad. Raf caught it when it was running toward you. Pretty cool, huh?"

Resnik noticed the rabbit was pretty big. "Amazing!"

Resnik's shoes were full of dirty water. He looked down at them while taking off his pack. He unzipped it and breathed out a sigh of relief. The contents had remained dry. "What do you say we head back. Are you guys hungry now?"

Both nodded. Resnik began the drudgery of walking back in soaked clothes and hiking boots but very thankful for avoiding being swept into the river. Having meat for dinner also became something to be grateful for.

A five-year-old catching a rabbit. Outrageous! He thought.

The rest of the forest would have to wait until next time. Getting clean and dry became the current priority, then making rabbit stew would round out this day.

The sound of three boys walking onto the front porch inspired Neko to leave her laptop and investigate. What a sight! She found Gettie looking up at her, anticipating his mom's reaction. Neko then stared at the rabbit in Raf's hand. Finally, her eyes moved to Resnik, looking him up and down incredulously.

He started taking off water-soaked, muddy hiking boots. "It's a long story, honey."

Neko remained speechless with her hands on her narrow hips.

Resnik gave Raf some directions. "Just leave the rabbit here so you can wash the blood off your elbows." He knew Gettie would go with him.

Resnik continued to disrobe, putting wet clothes in a pile on the porch.

"Leave those there, I'll get them after I start the shower," said Neko while watching him take off the last item, his boxer briefs.

She was tempted to join Resnik in the shower. Neko realized the boys could pop up at any time and besides, the wet/muddy clothes should be thrown into the washer.

When everyone was washed up, Resnik showed Neko and the boys how to prep the rabbit for supper. He added canned vegetables and chicken soup to create a stew. They all ate well that night. There were no leftovers.

The next morning found everyone in the house sleeping in a bit. Resnik was up first. He was thankful to find coffee, practically the only food item left. He brought a cup to Neko and set it down next to the bed.

"I'm going to the store to get some groceries. I'll be right back," he gave her a good morning kiss on her forehead.

Thirty minutes later, the entire house smelled like bacon. Five minutes after that, the four of them were at the table, eating a hearty breakfast.

"How about we all go on a hike today? We could get an early start!" Resnik shook off memories of getting wet the previous day.

That statement got the boys' attention. Neko simply gave Resnik a soft look and a nod of agreement. She realized sitting in front of a computer was a typical day. She was here to do the non-typical. Resnik grabbed a long stick with a three-pronged poker while the others got ready.

"What's that, Dad?" asked Gettie.

"It's a gig. I thought we'd try gigging frogs in the forest."

"Like stabbing them?" said Raf. He stared at the poker.

"Yeah, I thought since everyone liked rabbit, maybe we would also like frog legs. They taste just like chicken."

Gettie was the first to respond. "I'll try some."

The four of them made a beeline to the wooded area between the fields and river. It looked barren of leaves and almost scary. The forest was just beginning to bloom. The branches of oaks, cottonwoods, walnut, and others were extremely visible, not yet hidden by a green canopy. No two trees were alike. It seemed every possible shape of tree could be found. Most were gigantic in size. A truly ancient grove, untouched over time. The forest wasn't large in terms of square miles, although very concentrated with trees.

To walk through it was to tread on animal trails, mostly made by deer. The deer had cleared paths, making them safer. There were dangerous trees in the woods such as locusts and hawthorns that were full of incredibly long thorns. Poison vines could also litter the forest floor. The animal trails generally kept these annoyances at bay.

The four hikers set out to make a loop of the surroundings that encompassed the river, the forest, the railroad bridge, and the marsh. A daunting task for those who recently arrived from a city with low gravity. The ultimate goal was to make it to the railroad bridge. It's also the turnaround point. As they entered the forest, a plethora of smells met them. Not quite the greenhouse-ish odor of the Garden of Neom, but potent nonetheless. The river came next. Resnik's traditional lookout point was their first stop.

Everyone gazed at the slow-moving water. A few small turtles jumped off a log. No sightings of frogs yet. They walked along the high bank for a short distance until coming to several very large tree roots. The earth around these roots had been halfway washed out from previous floods. They looked ominous as they randomly wound about, creating sturdy fortresses while digging into the ground. The enormous trees that belonged to the roots were sentinels of an opening that leads out of the woods and into a field. As the four exited the forest, a little surprise awaited. A well-fed squirrel was standing alone looking for seeds in the newly planted field. Without hesitation, Raf was in pursuit. The squirrel took off toward the trees. Raf tried to intercept the squirrel so as to cut him off before losing him in the woods. Raf almost succeeded. The squirrel chose the nearest tree for refuge. Unfortunately for him, it was growing at an angle, not vertical like most of the other trees. Raf joined the bushy tail on the way up. With a leap, Raf caught his quarry by the neck. The effort caused him to become unbalanced. He had one hand around the squirrel and the other arm around the tree with his feet dangling. He was in a precarious situation. Resnik quickly ran to the rescue. He was just tall enough to reach up and wrap his fingers around Raf's feet. Resnik lowered Raf to his shoulders then squatted in order to reconnect Raf to the ground.

Raf then lifted the small creature to take a good look at his prize. The squirrel was lifeless. It had been inadvertently choked while Raf was struggling.

"That was crazy, bro," said an excited Gettie.

"Impressive, boy!" exclaimed Resnik.

Neko remained silent while putting her hand on Raf's thick white hair. She expressed herself by displaying a slight smile. Raf also smiled confidently.

"I guess we're eating squirrel tonight," added Resnik.

"Yes sir," Raf was proud of himself for being able to contribute something to the family that had given him so much. The fact is, he really felt part of the family.

After stowing the squirrel in the backpack, the four continued across the field to the bridge. It was customary to hike below the bridge before circling back and walking across it from the other side.

The bridge enabled two parallel sets of railroad tracks to cross over it. Past floods had created small gullies under the bridge and around its hundred-year-old supports. The water had made small dugouts safely above the large creek. Unlike the previous creek they had crossed, this one flowed swiftly all four seasons. Even in winter, it moved under the ice. It was also the cleanest water around, thanks to it running over a plethora of small rocks that fall off the bridge.

The four of them walked across, stepping on a few large stones. The embankment up to the bridge was steep. Neko's long legs enabled her to negotiate the angle. Resnik pushed up the boys in order to hand them off to her. Once up, they started to walk the tracks. The boys tried stepping on each railroad tie. Resnik and Neko walked beside the rails.

The reestablished marsh was the next destination on today's hike. They followed the tracks a relatively short distance until all four could oversee the freshly drained grassy area.

It looked sadly empty with just a trickle of drainage water moving through the middle. It smelled like clay slip one would use to adhere pottery pieces together. The marsh seemed to now be devoid of life— or at least visible life, though a frog or two could be heard, but not seen.

Too few to hunt. Squirrel will have to make do tonight, thought Resnik.

On the final leg of this morning's hike, the four adventurers walked between the rails of the tracks to avoid thick foliage on either side. As they approached the long driveway that led to the farm, something startled all four of them. A substantial-sized creature launched itself directly in front of them. Raf was tempted to run after it. The wild turkey was airborne in an instant and too fast for him. It left behind a large clutch of eggs. Raf moved toward the nest to pick one up.

"Better not, son, those are fertilized eggs and probably have developing chicks inside."

Raf had a puzzled look on his face as he pulled his hand back and stared at the nest. He desperately wanted what was in it but honored the advice of his surrogate father.

"If you cracked one open, it would most likely possess small feathers and an underdeveloped turkey fetus inside," added Resnik.

"Okay, sir," uttered a disappointed Raf.

They left the eggs alone but took a mental picture of the location so as to check on the hatchlings another time.

The Walking Encyclopedia

After the morning hike, an email awaited Resnik upon arrival back at the farmhouse.

"Hey, brother, are you still on Earth?"

It was Leal, Resnik's best friend.

Resnik replied, "Hey, cuz, I'm on the farm. Are you coming down?"

Leal had spent an inordinate amount of time working on Purgatory over the last many years. He had left a wife and daughter on Earth for long periods. Resnik knew it was inevitable that Leal would either have to cut way down on his time on the City in Space or bring his wife there. She had been struggling with health issues for most of their marriage. Annette stayed on Earth while their daughter finished school. Their daughter wanted to stay on Earth so as to be around friends. Now it was time to make a decision as to where Leal and Annette would make their full-time home. Resnik sensed the time was near for his best friend to make a choice. He was anticipating the next email entry to disclose such a revelation.

"Yeah, I'm coming down to get Annette. You wanna get together before I do that?"

"Definitely, I'll pick you up at the airport. Just let me know when."

Three hours later found Resnik and Leal sitting at the bar of a small-

town establishment drinking some beer.

"Still a little tough getting used to," said Leal between sips from his frosty mug.

"Beer?" questioned Resnik.

"No, Purgatory! I was in space a couple of hours ago now I'm in the land that time forgot."

Leal is a handsome man, every bit as tall as Resnik. In fact, when they were young and still growing, there was a continual banter between the two of them about who was the taller one. The two are the same height now, though Leal has always been more slender. The younger Leal also had thick dark-brown wavy hair. His now gray hair is contrasted by big brown eyes. Back in the day, the occasional girl was known to call them "bedroom eyes." There is wisdom and knowledge in that gray hair and, these days, a beard to match. Hence the endearing term Resnik has given him, "the Walking Encyclopedia." That name was appropriate to Resnik's best friend. Leal, being much more educated than his friend, has never denied any explanation that Resnik has put forth through the many years of their friendship.

Resnik took a sip from his own mug. "Yeah, it's pretty crazy." "How's your trip been so far?" asked Leal.

"Well, sometimes I think the terrain down here is more dangerous than space."

"The people as well," added Leal.

"So true, at least shadow beasts are straightforward. You know exactly what you're dealing with."

Before Leal replied, he displayed a concerned look on his face. "People on Earth can be deceptive." He spent time in the corporate world before devoting so much of his focus to Purgatory. "Have you watched any news down here?"

"Just a little, the local station. It has a smattering of global coverage."

"Can you trust it?" Leal looked up.

"You boys want another?" The barista offered the two lifelong friends more beer.

Really, the two of them were more than friends. A somewhat random DNA test revealed they are distant cousins. This was almost no surprise. As their close bond became elevated above all other friendships, a theoretical reasoning was taking place within Resnik's mind. The only way he could explain it to himself was to describe it as "two brothers from different mothers." Certainly, the analogy is accurate, if not physically possible. They are "family," though—maybe even a bit more. A platonic relationship that exceeds mere brotherhood.

Resnik declined. Leal ordered a vodka on the rocks.

"Not really, you have to read between the lines. Unfortunately, there seems to be no end to bias or even fake news."

Leal was stoic, showing no surprise while taking a drink from the glass that was just put in front of him.

Resnik attempted to lighten the mood by changing the subject. He also went to Leal's default: nostalgic thoughts. "Remember that glacier we climbed in the Rockies?"

"The one where we had only crampons and ice axes but no ropes.

Talk about deadly Earth terrain!"

"Talk about being young and dumb," Resnik reiterated.

"You were scared," Leal was fond of saying when recalling that particular adventure.

"Yes, I was. Do you think the Spirit was with us on that big hunk of ice?"

"Had to have been," said Leal.

"Yeah, definitely." In his mind's eye, Resnik recalled almost countless times when he should have been paralyzed or killed, on Earth and in space.

Leal raised his glass to take a drink. "You mean like that phantom who appeared and told you to build a city in space?"

"Not 'phantom,' a divine entity." "Wasn't it kind of ugly?"

"He appeared looking just like me," Resnik pointed to himself.

"Yeah, like I said."

"Ha, I think there's more than one out there."

"Like?"

"There's probably one designated for you, though he may be reluctant to transform," said Resnik facetiously.

"And why is that?"

"He'd be afraid to get stuck looking like you." Leal smirked.

Resnik rabbit-trailed once again. "Does Annette know you're coming?"

"Oh yeah, she's packed and ready to go."

Resnik thought for a second. "Why don't we all go back together to save *Ornan* an extra trip?"

"That would be efficient," noted Leal.

"More than that, I'm beginning to think *Ornan* is being scrutinized a little too closely these days."

"You mean like when it reaches Earth's atmosphere or while it's docked and recharging?"

"Both really, Guardian tech seems to be known worldwide at this point."

"Star tech," added Leal.

"Star tech…you mean Guardian tech?" asked Resnik.

"No, star tech. Someone let it slip that you said every planet, moon, and star is host to a Guardian. Each one harboring a specific form of technology. That person may have been the first to coin the phrase *star tech*," explained Leal.

Resnik was now feeling slightly violated. "And who are *they* saying is this someone?"

"The buzz is, that William guy whom you pardoned and removed from Purgatory."

Resnik shook his head up and down. "William Parti, I remember. He and his people attempted a coup by trying to launch me into open space."

Leal took his finger and his eyes off his Earth cell phone he'd been obsessing over. "How about we all meet up at *Ornan*'s charging station day after tomorrow?"

"I think we can do that. A venture in a tube to receive more Guar— star tech, will be the first priority once back on Purgatory," were Resnik's last words.

Levels

Only one window had light emanating from it as Resnik came quietly down the long driveway. His electric pickup was almost inaudible. He could tell the glow was coming from the master bedroom. Neko was waiting up for him. He could see her face reflecting light from her laptop screen. She looked totally focused, as usual.

I don't even think she's noticed me, thought Resnik.

He figured the boys were asleep. More thoughts of alone time with his beloved wife came to the forefront of his mind. Resnik exited the pickup and entered the house quietly so as not to wake Gettie and Raf. The old farmhouse stairs were a little creaky; he tried to tread softly. Resnik thought he might surprise Neko as he slowly opened the bedroom door.

"I heard you coming from halfway down the drive," said Neko without taking her eyes off the computer.

"Oh, you did?" responded Resnik in a playful tone. "Did you wait up just for me?"

"*Hai* [yes]."

She peeled back the sheet and blanket to reveal her unclothed body. The dim light flattered her slender figure. Neko turned the laptop screen toward her husband. The low light now captured him as he undressed. Her gaze became fixated on her handsome man. She had grown to count on special time with him. Though not a new act anymore, many subtleties were still being discovered. For Neko, joining with her man wasn't about how crazy they could make it. A high level of intensity and the 'closeness' that comes with it is where her passion lies. She couldn't have imagined such delight before Resnik. Nor did she really give any thoughts in that direction. Work was enough for her. Now her career pales in comparison to her very full life.

Dawn on the farm found Neko's back pressed up against Resnik's front. He had one arm around her and the other under her head. The sun was just starting to peek through the bedroom window.

"I'm not ready to wake up yet," uttered Neko in a barely audible voice.

"You mean *mezameru*?" Resnik offered her a Japanese substitute for the word "wake."

"Ah-ha."

As Resnik had gotten more proficient with Japanese, Neko gradually stopped using very much of it. She still had a small accent, but even that was fading. Resnik thought her confident, extremely feminine voice sounded delightful with or without an inflection.

"Do you feel like going back to Purgatory tomorrow?"

Definitely, I've been away from you and Gettie too long."

"You're going to miss Kurokaze," stated Resnik.

"I know. I love riding him and teaching him new things. I even like the way he smells." She grabbed Resnik's hand and held it to her chest. "The time may be getting close to bringing a large animal to our City in Space."

The woman of few words lay still and silent. "I've been meditating in preparation for our next voyage to receive star tech."

She broke her silence. "Star tech?"

"Yeah, Leal said that's the new catchphrase for Guardian tech. It kinda got stuck in my head. I think we should go into a tube as soon as possible."

"To learn how to bring a horse into space?" Her questioning voice had a hint of excitement in it.

"Yes, in part, but mostly how to make room for more people on Purgatory."

Another brief silence occurred. "Levels!" Neko spoke it in a clear, strong "wide awake" voice.

She turned to face Resnik, throwing a leg over him to initiate more special time.

Information

A cube in space connected to a round dome came into view. Annette had seen pictures of Purgatory and Neom; however, seeing them just floating in space was surreal. The square City in Space takes up just 1.5 miles of area, and the Garden of Neom doubles that area but in a round dimension.

The silhouette of these basic geometric shapes is impressive against the vastness of space, thought Annette.

They decided to bypass *Ornan*'s gate into Purgatory so as to offer Annette a wide view of the entire city. The triangle shape of their transport slipped through the thick atmospheric barrier. The protective walls are wide enough to completely encase *Ornan* for a brief instant while it enters the city. As it emerged, the scene unfolded. Annette's eyes were first drawn to the city center, which is substantial. She thought it mimicked a compact version of a typical downtown on Earth. At a closer look, gold streets could be seen leading to green space and a small waterfall. The river that emanated from there meandered through a grassy area and under a walking bridge into a small pond.

Leal pointed it out to his wife. "That's where sashimi fish are raised."

She was in awe! Annette noticed something else. "Is that a little farmhouse and windmill?"

Leal responded, "Yeah, that's where the Clayborns stay when they're not at the condo in town."

After the brief tour, *Ornan* landed on a dock surrounded by a small array of solar panels. The passengers were greeted by the personnel director, Summer Genosis. She had approved the entry of Annette previously, as she did with all who wish to visit or even live on Purgatory. It was time to meet her face-to-face. Summer was a large woman with Celtic roots. She was very talented. She could write a good story as well as play piano and sing. Her real gift was having a heart for people. Summer was able to see the true character in people. Her Earth history was counseling broken families and protecting children caught in the cross fire of sometimes angry, disobliging parents. Moving to Purgatory offered her solace from a continuously dysfunctional social system on her home planet.

"Welcome to Purgatory. How was your flight?"

A shapely woman with short hair cautiously and carefully walked out of the space shuttle. Annette's countenance began to improve with each step. The ninety-minute ride, along with the intense emotional experience of finally being in space, had taken a toll on her fragile health. However, feeling the lower gravity immediately improved the way she was feeling. An unexpected smile was starting to form on Annette's face.

She held out her hand. "Long," answered Annette. "But now that I'm actually here, much better."

Summer knew Annette's history; she shook her hand gently. "Let me show you our welcome facility."

The entire landing party, including the pilot, Wilson, made their way to the Kitchery. It was both welcoming and refreshing. They all chose to take full advantage of its accommodations. From the video screen/mirror that describes the city, to the plentiful variety of snacks, the Kitchery is almost a retreat instead of a starting point. One can even take a shower or simply plug in your device and relax inside a domed privacy chair.

Annette became energized after a short time at the Kitchery, though she needed to get to Leal's condo, her new home, to rest.

Resnik was anxious to get the crew together now that he was back on the city. With help from the Spirit within himself, he'd received coordinates for the next journey into a tube. The destinations were downloaded to his mind while he was relaxing on the trip up to Purgatory. That's usually how it worked. Resnik cleared the thoughts in his head and attempted to be at peace. This time was no exception. In fact, he was given not one destination, but three. He had several projects on his mind relating to the next journey and needed distinct technology for each. He was planning on engaging Neko, Makan, and Palmer for help.

Resnik set out to connect with Palmer and check on the status of *Derecho*, the vessel used to enter a tube. Mr. Clayborn reached for his Purgatory cell phone to order an electric car. It found its way to him within a minute. He left the others behind in order to drive across the city to the depot. This very well-equipped garage housed *Derecho*. Resnik knew he would find Palmer there, probably with greasy hands holding a tablet or laptop.

"Hello, son." As Resnik walked in, he immediately located Palmer under a city transport that was on a lift for repair.

"Hi, sir, did you just get back?" said Palmer while not taking his eyes off his work.

"Yeah."

"Let me guess, you're getting ready to go into a tube, and you want to know if *Derecho* is up for the task?" Palmer now looked in Resnik's direction.

"You guessed right!"

"And you need a pilot?" Palmer set down the electronic notebook he was holding.

"Right again," reiterated Resnik.

Palmer's Native American roots became more evident as time went by. The bold features on his face got more distinctive as he was approaching thirty years of age. His substantial nose, along with big green eyes, fit perfectly with bushy brows and long/thick brown hair. He displayed an easy-going smile to Resnik as he offered a handshake.

"Both *Derecho* and I are ready and willing."

Palmer's genius wasn't fully realized until he came to live on Purgatory. His focus on Earth was directed toward gaming and recreational substances. Resnik knew Palmer on Earth and pleaded with Summer to give him a chance. Besides one mishap, the choice to bring Palmer to the city has been exponentially beneficial to Purgatory. Receiving and utilizing the star tech that Resnik brought back to Purgatory seemed to always jump-start Palmer's thinking process. He viewed Resnik as a father figure, and Resnik was very fond of Palmer, like he was with his own son.

"Very good. Let's plan for tomorrow. I'll inform the rest of the crew."

He jumped back in the small electric car and made a beeline to Neom, a short distance from the depot. Resnik made sure to stick his head out of the window as he passed through the transition tunnel that joined Neom to Purgatory. Just past the air barrier was the potent smell of the Garden of Neom. The scent was of forest mixed with greenhouse, and no pollution residue. The aroma is that of new life. The humidity increased along with different sounds. Insects and frogs could be heard. Resnik was hoping to add birdsong to the mix soon. He looked for Yasti. Resnik figured she would be knee-deep in some sort of foliage. He was correct; there she was in a small field of green beans, holding a device. He exited the car to greet her.

They hugged. It was a meaningful embrace. They shared a bond. Each had saved the other's life on different occasions. That was actually Yasti's job (so to speak). She was tasked by a Messenger to watch over Resnik's life: kind of like a bodyguard. Being an entomologist had now become secondary. Her first priority was to make sure the founder/city director remained out of harm's way.

"Tomorrow, right?" Yasti could see the expression on his face. "I had a premonition."

"Yeah, of course, that's right. I'll text you the time to meet at the Hub."

"No later than 10:00 a.m.," replied Yasti confidently, as she gave a wink to Resnik.

"Yeah, right again. That's what I was thinking."

A secondary hug was exchanged, and Resnik was off to his high- rise office. He needed to connect with the Spirit privately, as he would before any journey or important situation.

He also wanted to connect with his array of colorful saltwater fish. To him, they represented beautiful heavenly bodies swimming in the vastness of space.

The city was beginning to dim to simulate the overnight cycle of Earth. Resnik turned in his desk chair to look out the floor-to-ceiling windows. The city looked glorious during a Purgatory night. The gold streets glimmered, the clear river water glistened, and the Garden of Neom glowed. The sun, planets, and stars could also be seen through the semitranslucent atmospheric walls. His emotions were stirred. Resnik imagined anyone who had the privilege of being there would also be in awe.

"Are you guys at the condo or riverside house?" texted Resnik.

Neko texted back, "In the condo, Raf went to Hera's condo."

"Be there in a few."

He was only a few blocks away. As Resnik arrived, he sought after Gettie. He kneeled down to look his son in the eye. "Are you glad to be back?"

"Yeah, but I kinda miss the farm and forest."

"I know. Would you like to go deeper in space tomorrow?"

"You mean like in one of those tube things?"

"Yes, and I can ask Raf's mom if he can go too."

Gettie's face lit up! "That would be cool, and Mom and you too?"

"Yep, all of us. There's a planet I want to show you."

Resnik glanced at Neko. Her big eyes were almost stern. "I'm sorry, honey, I should have asked you first."

She certainly trusted her husband with everything. Neko also trusted in Resnik's healing abilities to be utilized in the event of unexpected happenings. Withal, it had been years since any interstellar creature had come their way. She deemed taking the kids risky but beneficial.

The usual suspects were all there before 10:00 a.m. Even Palmer was there before ten, barely. He had a box of doughnuts in his hands, a much-desired ritual of a preflight tradition. Another requirement is to don a space jumpsuit. For the two young boys, it was simply warm jackets brought by Neko.

Yasti went to the wall of weapons to choose her favorite single-hand disruptors. She grabbed two and holsters to match. Neko picked her usual two-handed disruptor. Leal and Palmer chose one of each. Resnik picked out an air-saver bazooka just in case a smoke screen is needed.

"I see *Derecho* remains Vantablack," said Resnik to Palmer while stepping into the space vessel. "I see the PW is still intact."

Derecho looks like a cross between an antique VW bus and a bullet train. Palmer had applied his own symbol, PW (Palmer's Wagon), to customize the look of his favorite space vehicle.

Palmer replied, "I kinda got used to the black-out look, I like the stealthiness of it."

"Are you ready for an upgrade?" Resnik already knew what Palmer was going to say.

"Is that where we're going today, to finally get plans for a new *Derecho*?"

"That's one of our stops."

Leal overheard. "One of the stops?" He had a concerning tone to his voice.

That statement was hitherto not considered before this day. Standard protocol had been to land on only one heavenly body, receive valuable information from a Guardian, then return.

The possibility of varying from their routine raised some eyebrows. Neko gave Resnik a concerned look. Yasti seemed to have suspected this imperative.

Resnik spoke so everyone could hear. "We're actually making four stops today." He was confident and matter-of-fact in his tone.

The others respected his statement and took their seats. Palmer in the pilot's chair, Resnik as copilot. The boys in the first row, Neko right behind them. Yasti and Leal in the back two seats.

The white gate in the floor of the dock that held *Derecho* opened to allow the seven passengers to begin their interstellar journey. The two first-timers held on tightly to their seats with eyes glued to the windows.

Purgatory is located at a so-called crossroad of Guardian tubes. The initial tube to enter on this trip was Purge—kind of a main highway that leads to other tubes. Once through the portal, it took *Derecho* a few seconds to sync with the energy of Purge in order to enter. The two young boys held a little tighter as they subtly felt a slight vibration.

They were off and running! Speeding through a tube was very interesting to Gettie and Raf. Each one could be seen leaning a little as every planet, moon, or star passed by. The gravity of each interstellar body briefly tugged at the boys as *Derecho* crossed within their magnetic fields. Also, the corresponding light emanating from each star became a bit mesmerizing as their spacecraft steamed by them in the Guardian tube. Neko was hoping the boys wouldn't get sick. On the other hand, she actually found traveling in a tube relaxing.

The first stop was the planet Sedna (90377). Looking out of *Derecho*, it appeared reddish. The passengers could tell they were slowing down, not by the feel, but by the less frequent tugs and lights. A large illuminated tunnel was laid out on the surface. Palmer maneuvered their craft to the edge of the bright path.

Resnik turned to face the boys. "You guys stay here, seat belts on!"

Neko put a hand on each of their shoulders. Yasti became transfixed on Resnik, like a beloved canine intent on protecting her human. Resnik simply opened the door of *Derecho*, walked down its steps and onto the lighted path. Atmosphere and appropriate gravity were supplied. Someone was moving toward Resnik. At first glance, it looked like a brother. As the other individual got closer to Resnik, it looked like a twin brother. The glow in the tunnel made everything very clear. Those in *Derecho* could see Resnik's back, and the other Resnik's front. The two were even dressed alike. The boys became awestruck! Resnik and his twin just faced each other, and not for long. Before the boys had a chance to really reason this bizarre situation in their minds, it was over. Resnik turned back around and started walking toward the others. His twin walked in the opposite direction. The boys didn't know which Resnik to follow with their eyes. Gettie watched his dad, while Raf watched the mimic. The other Resnik just faded away. However, just before he disappeared, wings sprouted, and he got incredibly bright. Raf hit Gettie.

"Did you see that?"

Gettie quickly moved his gaze to Raf. "What?"

"Your dad… I mean that guy that looks like your dad turned into something else!"

Resnik reentered the cabin. He put his hands on the top of both boys' heads to reassure them.

"Everyone okay?"

Neko and both boys gave a small nod, the others started to relax as weapons lowered a bit. Resnik sat down next to Palmer, the tunnel dissipated, and they lifted off. Destination 2 was quickly underway. Traveling through Guardian tubes is extraordinarily fast, though a person really feels the distance. It can be exhausting traveling through space. As exciting as it is, the two young voyagers fell asleep after the next stop. Resnik's mind was filled to the brim after stop number 3, though he wanted to land on just one more planet, Super Earth (GJ357d). Palmer aimed for a body of water. Resnik woke the boys as they touched down next to a small lake.

"You guys wanna see somewhere even better than the forest?" Raf woke up first. "Yeah!"

Gettie heard Raf and opened his sleepy eyes.

"Zip up your jackets, it's a tiny bit cooler than Purgatory," Resnik initiated opening the hatch.

A beautiful clean breeze rushed into the cabin. It smelled every bit as clean as Purgatory, yet without the "new car" scent. Everyone took a deep breath; it was refreshing. The boys weren't the only ones ready to get up and move around.

It was an opportunity for the entire crew to explore. To this point, only Neko and Resnik had visited this planet, and that was six years previous. To their eyes, it looked the same, pristine.

Resnik took each boy's hand in his. "This is what Earth used to be like before a flood covered the entire planet, before roads and before great cities."

Gettie responded, "Can we go and check it out?"

"Sure," Resnik's eyes connected with Neko's. She could tell he had something on his mind.

Neko followed the boys to keep track of them, a disruptor slung over her shoulder.

Resnik gathered Leal, Yasti, and Palmer. "Did you guys see anything while I was connecting with a Guardian?"

During those first three stops, Yasti's eyes were glued on Resnik. Leal has a tendency to look behind. Palmer is much more likely to direct his attention to outer space.

Palmer spoke up. "Are you talking about a shadow? I thought maybe I was just seeing things."

"I glimpsed it too. I wasn't quite sure if it was real or just a figment," confirmed Resnik.

"Okay, so it was something, but what?" Palmer had a curious expression on his face.

"Did you happen to see it twinkle or gleam, maybe reflecting light from the tunnel?"

"Possibly, what are you thinking?" Palmer's big eyebrows were scrunched together, showing apprehension.

Resnik addressed his concern. "Years ago when we were fighting Dark Matter, a unique creature landed on the dome of Neom. He called himself 'Son of the Morning,' also known as Pride. The Guardians call him 'Son of Perdition.' The front of him is beautiful and sparkly, withal the back is Vantablack like *Derecho*."

"Black as a shadow, not soaking up any light!" said Palmer.

"That's right," answered Resnik.

The four were silent in contemplation. Leal spoke, "What's he up to?"

"I'm not quite sure. He is full of threats, that I know for sure. And he can be run off by Guardians."

"Is there a Guardian here?" asked Yasti.

Resnik answered, "Here on Super Earth, there is what Guardians call 'a Mighty One.' He is superior to other Guardians."

"That's a relief," said Leal.

"Just a side note, if you hear random music, don't keep it to yourself," The three of them stared at Resnik. "That's how Pride communicates. It all starts out pleasantly, like with your favorite music playing inside your head, but ends up with terrible and fearful sounds."

Resnik redirected his thoughts and looked around for his family plus one. He saw them literally petting some sort of animal. From an Earthling's perspective, it looked prehistoric. The creature possessed a horn on the middle of its head like a unicorn, had a humped back, and a short thick tail. From the distance Resnik was standing, he couldn't tell if the friendly animal had fur or scales. Suddenly, rising up from the water were huge heads. The necks that were attached got longer and longer. Then behemoth bodies began appearing above the surface.

"It must be a crater lake," said Resnik to his friends.

Yasti's yellow, animallike eyes were also locked onto the creatures. She still had two single-hand disruptors in their holsters. She thought about taking them out. Resnik noticed her hands moving toward the weapons.

"I think they're okay, Yasti, just curious."

He motioned for Neko and the boys to stay still; they were much closer to the water where the huge animals had emerged. The ground rumbled as the incredibly large animals were now walking on land. They passed by everyone on the way to a grove of trees.

"Pretty cool!" said Palmer as he looked up.

As the long-necked animals approached the trees, screeching could now be heard. No one really knew if the noise was birds, monkeys, or even both. The planet was certainly full of life. Resnik started getting hungry. He also had a head full of information to download into the Pillar. "Anyone else ready to get back and get some food?"

Raf sounded off first. "I'm hungry, but I want to see more."

"Yeah, this place is cool," said Gettie.

Resnik felt the boys had enough, at least for now.

"Let's go, guys," Resnik waved back Neko and the boys.

Everyone gathered themselves and loaded back into *Derecho*. Resnik fired a shot of aerogel out the aft end of their vessel in hopes of discouraging any unwanted entity from following.

"Was that better than the forest on Earth?" Resnik asked the boys as he came back to his copilot's seat.

"Way better, Dad," said an enthusiastic Gettie.

Raf followed with a "Yes sir!" He wanted to come back and run down one of those animals.

"Can we go back sometime?" asked Gettie.

"Yeah, we'll be back again," answered Resnik.

The crew (plus two) found their way in the tube Purge once again. They managed, without incident, to reach the portal that leads to the City in Space. As they exited the Guardian tube, Purgatory came into view. Something relatively small was moving across the atmospheric wall that faced the sun. It was an obvious blemish against the crystal- like appearance of that side of Purgatory.

"Leal, can you verify that's not our shadow?" asked Resnik.

Leal studied the relationship of the sun to *Derecho* and the proximity of the object. He wanted to be sure. "That's not us."

Palmer looked at Resnik. "Pride?"

Neko's questioning eyes were focused on her husband.

Resnik offered a statement of equanimity, "Let's hope he's not here for trouble, though it looks as if he's attempting to connect with someone."

"Connect?" asked Leal. "What do you mean?"

"Pride connected with my mind once when I was in Neom. He tries to initiate communication through emotions, usually dark emotions."

"Looks like he's found a victim," offered Leal while studying the creature that was latched onto the wall of Purgatory.

Resnik contemplated who that might be.

Derecho moved under the city toward the white gate of the depot. They could be vulnerable for a brief instant while they slipped through the gate barrier. Thankfully, Pride had other intentions at this time. All seven passengers were safe and sound, docked inside the depot.

The crew had just experienced a small reminder of the old days when battles with Dark Matter were more common. Appreciation of the safety within Purgatory would accompany their meal this evening.

"Hey, guys, I'm really full of information today. I've got to get over to the Hub and off-load this new tech. I'll meet everyone at Spazios." He knew the boys would love pizza to round out this adventurous day of travel.

Normally, Resnik could wait until the next day to input star tech within the Pillar. However, he had never received so much data in such a short span of time. He hopped on Palmer's electric motorcycle to get to the Hub fast. The Hub was a six-story building that houses the Pillar.

The Pillar was a very large six-sided computer that is the brain of Purgatory and Neom. It spans the full height of the building.

Resnik's typing ability wasn't the greatest, and he was anxious to meet the others, so he walked over to the corresponding stand-up desk to grab a small probe. He put the bean-sized device in his ear to connect to the Pillar. He simply thought back to the Pillar all the data he'd received. Resnik could feel it being transferred. When finished, he experienced a sense of relief and accomplishment. His stomach now became the top priority.

Resnik arrived at the restaurant just in time to offer a traditional premeal salutation.

"What a day! We were reminded of how much we have to be thankful for! This new tech will keep us busy for quite a while and take Purgatory to the next level. We now have information for a new *Derecho*, a way to process large animal waste, a way to make more room for additional people up here, and even help Makan to make it rain in Neom. Exciting opportunities for everyone on the City in Space!"

The Girl under the Bridge

An adorable young petite woman could not hide her protruding abdomen, not even with her long light brown hair. This first-time pregnancy made her feel a little self-conscious. She couldn't make herself buy maternity clothes either. Kassi just wore some of her loose-fitting garments. Being a conservative dresser made that option easy. She had her hands full, schooling the two twelve-year-old boys. They were much more challenging than being pregnant. And very rewarding, too. Kassi wouldn't say it out loud; however, Gettie and Raf were her favorite students. She wanted to stay working as long as possible just to be involved in their lives. The word *work* was an understatement. At times, the boys challenged her intelligence quotient. What one didn't know, the other did. Even when they had their own individual assignments, they helped each other. Kassi had never seen anything like them. They were a team.

Both were handsome young men, though Raf was now many inches taller than Gettie. The contrast between them was still great, Gettie being a light-colored pretty boy and Raf a dark-complected stately young man.

Raf's mother, Hera, was proud of her son. Most of the fear she felt about an offspring from Raf's father was subsiding. Azazel was his name. At one time in his ancient past, he could transform himself into a handsome man. When she last saw Azazel, his body was that of an appalling creature, though his true form was angelic. Hera just wanted her baby to look human. And if possible, not to be an evil/power- seeking being like his father. Hera found relief from her fears in seeing Raf thrive on Purgatory. She was also satisfied witnessing her son spend so much time with Resnik and his family. Hera always knew a son from Azazel would be strong. She also knew Raf would need someone stalwart to mentor him. Hera loved Raf; however, she was glad to sacrifice time with him so that Resnik can father him.

Gettie was also growing up and making his parents proud. Neko considered Gettie the most beautiful thing she'd ever seen. For her, that was saying a lot. She loved Resnik. He was very different from every male she grew up around in Japan. Tall, blond, and strong. She'd learned to really appreciate those physical attributes, being taller than average herself. Beyond visual attraction, Neko fell in love with Resnik's heart. She also fell in love with a horse named Kurokaze. The beauty of the City in Space (that she designed) and space itself all filled her heart, but in Neko's mind, Gettie's personality and appearance were the most magnificent! She could see Resnik and herself in Gettie. Maybe a little more of Resnik than her, but it mattered not; she loved both of her guys.

The time had come for another Earth visit. The boys, now young men, needed to reconnect with Earth's gravity and fill their lungs with heavier, less pure air. Raf had been chasing down some of the new animals that were brought into Purgatory. Most of the time it was catch-and-release, but he needed new challenges. Even with more people arriving to live on the city, Gettie longed for new faces that were his age, preferably female.

It was late summer on Earth. Resnik deemed it a good time of year for the young men to experience the humidity and heat of planet Earth. They were so used to the ideal climate of Purgatory. Resnik thought it was time to toughen up Gettie and Raf. He felt the change of atmosphere would benefit himself as well. Neko still periodically spent time in the desert air of Alulu; she was probably the most fit of all.

Resnik met the young men at school. It appeared Kassi was ready to give birth at any time; her baby bump was substantial. He figured she needed a break from Gettie and Raf.

"Thanks for hanging in there so long. I'm going to get these guys out of your hair for a while," offered Resnik.

Kassi looked relieved. "I probably need a break. I'm due in a few days!"

"You've been awesome! The boys really love you. You've been good for them."

"And they've been good for me. I hope my boy grows up to be like them." Her hands were rubbing her large baby bump.

Resnik turned to face the young men. "Tell Mrs. Pagoni thanks."

They both did as they were told.

Resnik smiled at the boys. "You guys wanna get out of here?"

"Yes, sir!" exclaimed Raf.

"You mean Earth?" said Gettie.

"Yeah! *Ornan* is ready to go."

"What about our clothes and stuff?" asked Gettie.

"We'll go shopping on Earth!"

Their faces lit up. Purgatory's market carried basic items, but nothing like the variety found in a large Earth city. Besides, the two young men wanted the latest styles befitting teenage boys. They had thoughts of coming back to Purgatory as the best-dressed fellas there. This flight would take the three of them to *Ornan*'s charging station in California, then an Earth jet to Omaha, followed by a small electric airplane to the small-town airport, close to the farm. Neko would meet them there.

Cobwebs lay in wait for the space travelers. The farm and its surroundings were very alive this time of year. That included bugs of all kinds. Birds as well were fluttering about. Resnik was dive-bombed by barn swallows who had nested on the front porch. In fact, there were two nests above the front door.

"How about we start getting acclimated right away? If we go on a short hike now, we should be back before Miss Neko arrives." As always, the two young men were up for a challenge.

Off they went. The fields were almost completely ripe at this time of year. The three fellows began the hike by circumnavigating the cornfield. The height of the stalks was well over Resnik's head. Up the driveway and along the tracks was the only clear pathway. That way was a little shorter as well, which was fine with Resnik on this first day back to stronger gravity.

Train activity seemed to be at a minimum this afternoon. They passed the marsh to find it devoid of water but very green. A small, lone, abandoned beaver dwelling could be seen. It stood out as the only point of interest in the one-time pond. They continued walking. The train bridge now came into sight. The distant whistle of a train got their attention. They quickly stepped off the tracks just before the bridge to cross the creek below. The deafening rumble of train cars was just feet away. The guys could feel the ground shake. The moving train commanded their gaze. As they looked up from under the bridge, something else caught their eyes. They all saw it and froze. Raf stopped midway across the creek, standing on a big rock. The distraction that caught their attention looked like the head of an animal. Its hair was like a tangled mop. The three waited to ascertain if it was alive. This creature had nestled in one of those dugouts, protected from rain and sun by the bridge above it.

The fast-moving train finished crossing; silence took over. Gettie made a splash crossing the creek while trying to join Raf, who stood sentinel like a dog on point. The noise of the water splashing roused the hairy thing. Its head looked up. The eyes looked human; the face was too dirty to tell for sure if it was a person or a beast. Suddenly, it started running on two legs, away from the hikers. In a nanosecond, Raf followed. It had the edge over Raf. He was already fatigued and not used to the heavier gravity. The scared creature lost him quickly. Outrunning Raf was a rare occurrence. He came back frustrated.

"Don't be too hard on yourself, son," Resnik attempted to console Raf. "Sometimes animals run in the opposite direction of their dwelling to throw off a pursuer. There's still plenty of light; let's do a 180 and see if we can track it." He gave Raf a pat on his back. "Good try."

The forest was in full bloom at this point. They picked up a well-worn but vague trail that led from the creek. Resnik couldn't tell if it was made by a two-legged or four-legged animal. They went east, away from the creek and toward the river. The three of them scrutinized the trail, looking for tracks, poop, or even discarded bones. The path seemed to be in a somewhat straight line. They diligently walked about 1/8th of a mile with eyes wide and ears open. Resnik could now smell the river, which marked the end of the trail. A hint of discouragement began creeping into his emotions. He tried not to let it show. The riverbank was now in view as the path ended.

A heavy sigh came out of Resnik, and the two young men heard it. All three stopped and stared at each other. As Resnik glanced downward toward the boys, he saw something. He put his finger over his lips and pointed silently at the ground with his other hand. A few small feathers could be seen. Upon closer scrutiny, they found small bird bones. All three squatted down and very quietly searched the forest floor for more indications of leftovers. The only point of interest in the vicinity was an oversized ancient tree that had broken and partially fell into the river. It had grown close to the edge of the bank and remained attached to its trunk. It fell over because it was hollow. The remaining part of the tree was about five and a half feet high. Resnik figured the stump was also hollow.

Looks like a mother tree, thought Resnik.

He was planning on looking inside. With more silent hand motions, he indicated to Gettie and Raf his intentions. Their searching eyes were focused on his every move. He gave a slight nod, and the boys understood. Resnik counted down on his fingers: *Three...two...one*. He slowly peeked over the rim of the hollow stump. A sharpened stick glanced off his forehead. He then quickly grabbed it. Raf came over and was just tall enough to see inside for himself. They couldn't believe what they were looking at! A scared little girl was staring at them. She was hunkered down, helpless and trapped. She peered back at four eyes connected to blond hair and white hair. Her own hair was a matted mess; it kind of looked brown, but it was difficult to tell. She looked half-starved.

"It's okay, we're not here to hurt you. You can come out. We have food," said Resnik.

That statement wasn't altogether true. Resnik and the two young men left Purgatory in a hurry; he was planning on going out for dinner that night. It was probably their most inept preparedness ever.

After hearing the pleasant tone of Resnik's voice, she thought about standing. Also, Resnik's face seemed somewhat familiar to the scraggly girl.

"Can we help you out of there?" asked Resnik.

With some extra effort, she managed to climb out herself. Resnik was afraid she might run. She thought about doing just that. Suddenly she saw Gettie. He was about her height. The young girl froze; her heart melted! She was tired from running and weak from malnutrition; her knees started giving out. Resnik caught her before she hit the ground. As he held her, he could feel her distraught emotions as well as her physical weakness. The wild girl fainted.

Of all the times we go hiking, and this time we don't bring any food!

He thought.

He gently sat her down and put his hand on her forehead. He uttered soft, unperceivable words. After a few moments, the girl came to. She opened her eyes once again to find Gettie, who was now squatting down next to her, holding her hand. She was leaning against Resnik's knee, still speechless.

"I'm Gettie. Do you have a name? Can you talk?"

The feral girl stuttered, "I...I...I'm Isha."

Resnik chimed in, "We're all glad to meet you, Isha." His voice soothed her once again. "Can you stand?"

Isha felt surprisingly stronger after sampling Resnik's healing ability.

"Y-yes, I...I think so."

"This is Raf," indicated Resnik.

She looked up at the tall young man, then her eyes quickly returned to the handsome boy holding her hand.

"You're very special to manage outrunning Raf." Resnik was lightening the mood.

"Let's get you some food. Is there anything here you want to take along?"

"I...I don't h-have an-anything," Isha then reconsidered, looking around. "Ma-ma-my stick."

Gettie quickly grabbed it and handed it to her.

"That thing works pretty good," added Resnik with a sarcastic smile on his face, he had blood dripping down his forehead.

Isha remained stoic as if she didn't really hear him. As Isha started walking, she reached for Gettie's hand. He gladly gave it to her once again.

At least I remembered my Earth cell phone, thought Resnik. "Hey, honey, are you close? Do you need a ride?" He texted Neko.

She sent a quick reply, "Pick me up in thirty mins."

Resnik figured it would take about that much time to get back. "Hey guys, I might run ahead so I can meet you at the tracks with the pickup. Raf, take care of them for me."

This was such an honor for him. To have Resnik's trust was a privilege. "Yes, sir," responded Raf with enthusiasm.

Resnik may have been a little overconfident about hurrying to fetch the truck. After twenty steps, his muscles were in serious oxygen debt. With great effort, he managed to retrieve the truck in a timely manner. He was still out of breath as he met the three children just exiting the tracks and onto the driveway.

He motioned to Gettie, "Hop in, we've got to get your mom."

Isha seemed compliant while in Gettie's care. She got in without issue.

The sunset was directly behind Neko as they saw her walking down the country road. The small-town airport was only a mile from the farm.

"Hey, good-looking, you need a ride?" Resnik reached over to open the passenger door for Neko.

She stopped in her tracks. Resnik was still breathing hard with blood on his face, and there sat a stranger holding her baby boy's hand, and this girl had a spear. The strange girl smelled bad and looked worse. The stink caused Neko to be hesitant. She overpowered her sense of smell and decided to get in while giving Resnik her signature WTF look. The woman of few words had none to utter.

Resnik spoke, "Honey, meet Isha. Isha, this is Mrs. Clayborn. You can call her Miss Neko."

A "little girl" sound came from the back seat, "Ca-Clayborn, R...Are you Ra-Resnik?"

Everyone in the truck was astonished!

Neko turned to face Isha. "Do you know who he is, honey?"

"I…I've been la-la-looking for ha-him."

The country road was close to town. Resnik pulled into the nearest restaurant parking lot; it was Mexican food this night.

Resnik leaned over and whispered to Neko, "Let's talk while we get Isha some food."

Isha left her stick in the pickup so she could hold Gettie's hand with both of hers. Once everybody settled into a booth, Isha relented one of her hands so as to eat. Gettie managed eating with only one of his hands as well.

They all did more eating than talking. Isha initially ate ravenously, then slowed; she got full fast. Neko sat quietly, studying Isha. Neko grew up being a skinny slender girl, which was natural for her. She wondered how natural it was for Isha to be so thin. Neko wanted to get Isha to the farm and clean her up.

Everyone had questions for Isha; however, they let her eat in peace. Patience would be the rule this evening. A stop at the grocery store after dinner was warranted. Isha was still clinging to Gettie. He had never held a girl's hand before, besides his mother's. *What a difference*, he thought. That simple act stirred feelings inside himself the didn't know he had. Isha's hand is smaller than his. He felt strong holding it; Gettie possessed big hands like his father. An adrenaline rush overcame him when Isha first touched him.

His senses were bombarded. The sound of her feminine voice tickled his ears. The wave of energy from her slender body could be felt going up his arm. Gettie could "feel" her attraction to himself, and he was attracted to her. He was able to look past her dirty neglected appearance. He saw in her someone underfed but strong and fast.

She is a survivor, he thought. Isha was independent and brave, yet in an instant, she chose him as someone she could rely on. Sexual desires were fired up as well. Gettie wanted more of her, to hold her and get to know her, even take care of her.

Resnik urged Isha to pick out anything she might want or need. "We have plenty of cupboard space; in fact, the cupboards are bare. We could use some help filling them, so grab whatever."

Neko made sure to get plenty of shampoo and soap if Isha failed to do so. Neko also loaded age-appropriate feminine products into the cart, just in case.

Isha was in shock! She was driven by need. She had been cold, hot, hungry, scared, lonely, dirty, and above all, desperate. As long as she could hold something tangible, that would keep her grounded and focused. Gettie was that security. Without thinking, Isha identified his worthiness instantly. She made her choice deep inside her heart. Isha couldn't explain it to anyone or even to herself. She just knew, and Resnik's healing seemed to reaffirm her decision to choose Gettie.

As she walked down the grocery aisles, Neko stared at the two hands that had become one. To this point, only her hand had held Gettie's. She was flabbergasted! Resnik couldn't help noticing his wife's big eyes glued on the two youngsters. He came to the rescue by putting his hand around hers. Neko had tears forming while watching her little boy's attention turn to another.

Raf was now in front, leading the two couples down the aisles. He was also in shock! His best friend and surrogate brother had become enthralled by another, and of all people, a feral girl! Incredibly strong emotions were also confronting him. He felt betrayed; Gettie was *his* rock, not Isha's. Raf didn't know who to blame for his pain, this stranger or his surrogate brother. Raf had heard Resnik talk about the Spirit. Was the Spirit what he needed now? He felt anger beckoning. That feeling, he knew. Why didn't he have his own dad? Why was his paternal ancestry talked about in hushed tones, like a dark revelation? Once he bought into anger, jealousy showed up. Then envy came along for the ride, followed by malice. A slippery slope of dark emotions entered Raf's heart. He was introduced to a destructive mood this day, and he couldn't shake it. However, he could hide it; Raf had seen his mom do that. From now on, Raf would assume the role he'd seen Resnik and Gettie perform so well. He had been the instigator; now he would be a leader!

The pickup bed was filled with food and essentials. Many grocery carts had contributed to the excess. Once back at the farmhouse, Resnik backed up the truck close to the porch steps.

"Okay, boys, please take everything in," requested Resnik.

Gettie and Isha were still attached. They tried to help carry stuff in by each grabbing an item with their free hand. Raf became disgruntled. He was unmotivated, yet he let anger give him energy.

"I got it. You guys can go in." Even at this age, Raf had a big sound in his voice.

Gettie and Isha did as requested.

Neko began rifling through a drawer in the bathroom, looking for some trimmers she may have come across at some point. *Ah-ha*, she thought. She handed them to her husband. "Can you please help?"

He knew what Neko wanted. "Honey, we'll set up in the kitchen."

Isha and Gettie sat together at the large island countertop in the kitchen. Resnik was armed with electric trimmers. Isha allowed him to examine her messy hair. "Isha, I think your hair is done for. I believe there are things growing in it."

Neko confirmed, "Honey, I won't be able to get a comb through it. Can we cut it?"

Isha was initially dismayed. She put her free hand up to feel how bad it was. She had just been given more than she could have dreamed of, even against that very morning. Her stomach was full; she was now sheltered and safe. And she had her new friend by her side. She decided to forgo her hair. Isha's big eyes looked up to Neko as she stuttered, "Ya-ya-ye-yes."

Neko tried to reassure Isha, "It'll be okay."

The nasty hair started to fall to the kitchen floor. Neko attempted to catch as much of it as possible, immediately putting it into a plastic grocery bag for quick disposal.

As Resnik cleaned up the stubble on her head, he came across an almost imperceptible square protrusion. There was a practically unnoticeable scar going down the center. He glanced at Neko, who had her big eyes locked onto it. She was tempted to touch it but held back, thinking Isha may be ignorant of its existence.

"You have a pretty head, honey," said Neko.

"Yeah, it looks cool," added Gettie.

Isha smiled bashfully. "Ya-ya-you're th-the m-m-most be-beau-utiful boy I-I've e-ever seen!"

The kitchen went dead silent! Gettie's creamy white skin went red. Neko covered her mouth. Resnik wore a proud smile. Raf's emotions were again thrown into turmoil. Isha kissed him on his cheek, tears flowing down her face. Neko hugged Isha from behind and kissed her bald head. "Let's get the rest of you cleaned up, honey." She took Isha's free hand to lead her to the bathroom. "Gettie won't be able to take a shower with you, but I'll stay in the bathroom, if you want?"

Isha nodded, she reluctantly released Gettie's hand.

Neko called out to Resnik. "Babe, can you bring down some of my clothes that might fit Isha?"

"When was the last time you took a shower?" asked Neko.

"B-before I…got o-on th-the t-train."

"You mean one of the trains that go by here?"

They were talking through the shower curtain.

"Ya-yes," replied Isha.

Neko figured that was enough conversation for now. When the water stopped, she handed Isha a towel over the top of the shower curtain. "Do you want me to leave so you can get dressed?"

Isha poked her head around the curtain and simply shook her head no.

A pile of Neko's clothes were waiting for Isha just outside the bathroom door. To Neko's eyes, looking at Isha was like looking in a mirror nearly thirty years previous, a skinny twig of a girl. Every item of clothing that had been brought down was oversized and baggy, though Neko found a way to secure them upon Isha.

"Do you want something to keep your head warm?" offered Neko.

Isha nodded. Neko called to her son. "Gettie, please bring me a hat."

He immediately fetched his stocking cap, which was hanging by the front door. Isha put it on. She was clean. She smelled good. She was wearing his favorite hat. Isha was the cutest, most desirable thing he'd ever seen. He wanted to hold more of her than just her hand and possibly return a kiss. He was timid and unsure of what to do. He would settle for her hand for now.

"Ha-how d-do I la-look?"

Gettie tried to downplay his excitement but couldn't hold back. "Amazing!" he said with a gleam on his face.

Isha smiled with more enthusiasm than she could ever remember! She'd brushed her dingy teeth after her shower. They looked surprisingly brilliant as she displayed her emotions by smiling uncontrollably.

Witnessing this exchange brought some fear to Neko. She learned the dynamic of love and attraction from her relationship with her husband. Seeing it played out before her eyes between Gettie and Isha was too much. *They're so young.* She felt Gettie's father was needed. Neko knew Resnik had been without parental guidance growing up. That unstructured state of affairs seemed to allow him to go down a path of bad decisions. She wanted much better for her son and knew her husband did as well. She was hoping Resnik would have a talk with Gettie.

When it came time to shut everything down and sleep, another precarious situation presented itself. Where to put Isha? She was used to sleeping in a tree or under a bridge. Neko stepped up to the challenge once again. She sat on the couch next to Isha, who was sitting next to Gettie, holding his hand. Neko grabbed Isha's free hand.

"Isha, why don't you sleep here on the couch?" She then looked at Gettie. "Honey, your father wants to talk to you, alone."

Gettie reluctantly let go of Isha's hand and joined his father in the kitchen. "Yeah, Dad?"

"What a treasure we found in the forest today," he started. Gettie nodded. "Yes, sir."

"You know what it means to be a gentleman, right?"

"Yes, I remember." Gettie's young gray eyes were looking up at Resnik's older and wiser gray eyes.

"And you know what it means to have good character, right?" Gettie nodded again.

"Isha is very vulnerable. She's chosen you. She needs you. That's a big responsibility! I need you to slow things down. Be there for her, but don't rush ahead even though you want to, okay?"

"Okay, but I really want to, Dad. I get so worked up when she talks to me. I don't even care if she stutters. I kinda like it."

"I know, son, that's natural. And it's okay for you to like her back. It's also okay for you to hold hands. I can tell she really needs that right now. Just don't let it go further than that."

"Okay, Dad." Inside his heart, Gettie didn't want to go slow. He'd never felt this way before. New emotions and physical feelings were surfacing! However, he agreed to honor his dad's request.

Resnik offered his hand to Gettie so they could shake on it and close the conversation. The two of them then reentered the living room.

Resnik focused his attention on Isha, who was still sitting with Neko. "Isha, we're so glad we found you today! You're welcome to stay with us as long as you like. In fact, we were all planning on going shopping tomorrow for clothes and stuff." He gave Neko a wink (this plan was news to her). "We would love it if you would go with us."

Isha smiled and nodded.

Resnik continued, "Can you sleep here on the couch tonight, by yourself?"

Tears started forming in her eyes. Neko immediately put an arm around Isha.

Resnik quickly offered a solution. "How about Gettie stays here in the living room on a chair?" He gave Gettie a quick glance. "And Raf will take the other chair." He stretched out his arm to indicate Raf, who was already sitting on the chair.

She nodded once again.

"Okay, that's all settled. I'll leave the kitchen light on. Raf, can you get pillows and blankets for everyone?"

Raf was so ready to do something. He was having a hard time keeping a lid on his frustration.

Clothes, Shoes, and Secrets

The next morning found Raf snuggled in his chair, Isha on the couch, and Gettie on the floor with his back up against the couch, holding Isha's hand which was drooping over. Neko deemed it precious, while Resnik was more cautious with his evaluation of the situation. Gettie's hat had slipped off Isha's head during the overnight. Neko gently planted a soft kiss on Isha's bald head then carefully replaced the hat.

The morning started with coffee for Neko. Resnik prepared a hearty breakfast, anticipating three hungry kids.

Leaving for the big city was easy and straightforward. For the most part, everyone just had the clothes on their backs, except Neko, who seemed to have stashed clothes in multiple locations. After breakfast, they all loaded into the pickup for the thirty-minute drive to Lincoln. Isha was wearing a pair of Gettie's old farm shoes; her worn-out shoes were taken to the burn pile. She looked like a vagabond with her baggy clothes, overlarge mud-crusted shoes, and a stocking hat with no visible hair poking out. Of course, she *was* a vagabond, or at least until today. Neko had big plans to fix up Isha. She completely embraced Isha as a surrogate daughter, the way Resnik had practically adopted Raf. And what a deal, instead of being the only female among three males, the balance was improving. Neko could hardly wait to spend the day with Isha.

"Isha, can I take you with me while the boys go shopping for guy stuff?"

Isha froze for a moment, a worried look came upon her face. Neko offered Isha a hand to hold.

Gettie chimed in. "It'll be okay. Mom is awesome! She'll take care of you."

"It's fine, honey. We'll check on each other frequently," offered Neko, showing Isha her cell phone.

Isha looked up at Neko with her incredibly pale-blue eyes. Isha appeared so different on this new day. They were at the outdoor mall with the sun shining. Isha's exceptionally long eyelashes could now be easily seen. Her tan skin held very subtle freckles. Isha's sweet fragile demeanor touched Neko's heart. *How could this little angel survive in the wilderness on her own?* thought Neko. She was hoping this day with Isha might also reveal answers to this mystery.

Isha turned back to Gettie to give him a meaningful hug. It didn't last long. Gettie was caught off guard. He didn't have a chance to hug her back before it was over. He had to just watch her walk away with his mom. It was like witnessing his mom holding hands with a little pretty clown.

Resnik breathed a sigh of relief. He wasn't aware of his son ever holding a girl before. Resnik thought it may have been system overload for Gettie.

Resnik noticed the shock on Gettie's face. In his mind, he thought, *Glad that didn't last very long.* "Okay, son, shake it off, we've got stuff to do," he said to Gettie.

Resnik noticed Raf was maybe a bit more quiet than usual. "How you doin', Raf?"

"Okay, sir," replied Raf. He was now slipping into a role of duplicity to hide his torn emotions.

Neko and Isha periodically showed up to connect with the three boys. Each time, Neko had a bigger bag of goodies. It seems Isha would see something interesting to eat, then just take one or two bites before she was full. This time, Neko gave the bag to Raf. He looked inside. There were pretzels, cookies, miniature doughnuts, etc. Neko needed to off-load as much as possible in order to carry the bulk of new clothes and shoes for Isha. Gettie became hypnotized looking at Isha. She had a stylish pair of Converse shoes on her feet, a new feminine hat on her head, and clothes that fit perfectly.

Gettie looked her up and down, fascination written all over his face. "You're the coolest girl I've ever seen!"

She was beaming! While Gettie was gawking, Neko gave Resnik a kiss and whispered in his ear, "I've got a lot to tell you." She'd been patiently listening to Isha all day. Much history of the mysterious "girl in the forest" had been revealed. It went slow because of the stuttering. In Neko's mind, one or two more stops would be prudent to reveal more secrets.

The young men were sporting new clothes as well. Keen shoes were on their feet, and Kuhl shirts and pants covered their bodies. Sunglasses were also on the list, as the unfiltered sunshine on Earth could be harsh on unprotected eyes. Eating supper became the next challenge.

What does Isha like to eat? Resnik pondered, *And where could they go to sit separately from the kids?* He wanted to hear what Neko was learning from the girl who had won her heart.

Isha was in the mood for an old-fashioned burger and fries. Resnik urged Gettie to share with his new best friend, knowing she wouldn't eat much. The three kids ate in a separate booth. Raf once again had to tough it out. He felt alone while the young couple shared their meal. Neko was excited to finally get the opportunity to get her husband caught up concerning Isha. "Does she have parents? Do they need to call the police? Why was she looking for Resnik?" He became all ears. Resnik didn't have to wait long. The woman of few words was ready to spill the beans, perhaps communicate more than she'd ever done. It seemed Isha was on the run. "She came from California. She's running away from her father. The mother is unknown. Her father's name is A. L. Sek."

Resnik actually knew that name. When Dan Gater of Epygen died, A. L. Sek took over as CEO. Epygen used to be a major sponsor of Purgatory until Gator tried to ice Resnik by releasing him into open space.

Isha hitched rides on trains to arrive in Nebraska. She overheard her father talk about Resnik and Purgatory and that there was a farm in the Midwest. She dug deeper and narrowed it down to Nebraska. Isha felt trapped in California; she discovered that experiments were going to be performed on herself. She began to wonder what else was going on at Epygen.

"Her father is cold, calculating, and distant. She started thinking of herself as a project, not a daughter. Isha began following you on social media. She ascertained that Resnik must be some sort of healer. To most of the world, that attribute was underplayed, dismissed as a rumor. After all, who could do those things people gossip about? However, Isha believed."

"A twelve-year-old girl hitching all the way from California?" reiterated Resnik.

"I know!" Neko was also amazed.

"We need to look into this further," said Resnik. "Dan Gater was evil. Sounds like Epygen is up to their old tricks."

Neko remembered well. She's the one who got launched up toward outer space while saving Resnik. A Guardian rescued her in the nick of time.

Resnik made a bold decision. "Let's keep a lid on this until we get back up to Purgatory. I know Dr. Alexandria and the Pillar can shed some light on all of this."

Neko gave her signature nod.

"Thanks for taking care of Isha today, honey! Seems like you're her only mom, and you're so good at it."

"I already love her!" Neko had tears in her catlike eyes.

He kissed her forehead. "You better eat. I've never heard you talk so much! Aren't you hungry?"

"Just need a couple of bites. I sampled some of Isha's snacks so she wouldn't feel odd."

Resnik got up to go sit by Raf. "You guys in the mood for a movie?"

Purgatory now has a movie theater, though it can't get the newest films. Resnik thought everyone might like to see a "fresh" release. Three enthusiastic thumbs-up were raised. The movie *The Way of Water* was their next stop.

After the movie, Resnik started wondering if they should shorten this visit to Earth. His mind was swimming with thoughts of Isha and her journey. "She seems so needy, yet incredibly brave and tenacious." His first inclination was to believe that Isha wanted to be loved but didn't know what it was. *She's never been loved!* He thought. "Yet she has so much love to give."

"Hey, honey, do you want to go back up to Purgatory tomorrow?"

Resnik could have guessed her answer. Neko had already been on Earth for a while.

She spoke quickly. "With Isha?"

"Yeah. I want to get to the bottom of these secrets. How did she find her way here without a cell phone or device? What's Epygen up to now? Stuff like that."

Neko simply gave a slight nod as she smiled in agreement.

The farm was a pleasant sight after a full day in the big city. Gettie helped Isha bring in her "large haul" of clothes and shoes. The young men also got hooked up with gear as well, but they didn't have the abundance of stuff that came from the favor of Miss Neko.

"C-c-can I-I sh-show you all my…my new things?" Isha asked Gettie.

"Yeah, that'll be fun. I'll be right back."

Gettie eased his hand out of hers and left Isha on the couch so he could go to the bathroom. When he returned, she was sound asleep. Lights went out at that point, except in the kitchen. Gettie boldly assumed his spot on the floor, while Raf curled up in his favorite chair. Neko gathered all of the day's trappings and packed them for tomorrow's flight. Resnik made arrangements with his pilot friend Wilson to bring *Ornan* the next day. He also notified a slightly confused Summer of the "stowaway," Isha.

The electric airplane was loaded to its weight limit this early morning. Isha looked adorable in her second new outfit. She was settled in the airplane seat, as happy as can be to have the chance to visit the City in Space along with her new friends.

Discoveries

Isha's pale eyes were open wide as the pearl-white gates of the city came into view. She counted three: one for the Garden of Neom, one for the depot, and the third, called the City Gate. Wilson chose the third gate. Coming into Purgatory through the atmospheric barriers was a bit tricky now that the second level to the city had been established.

Gettie was excited to show Isha the Kitchery. He led her in so she could indulge within the spa-like facility. True to form, Isha was only in the bathroom long enough to relieve herself. The extravagant amenities couldn't entice Isha; being alone upset her too much. She did grab a snack and a bottle of water. She took only one bite of the protein bar but drank almost all the water in a succession of continuous swallowing.

"The-that wa-wa-was the ba-ba-best wa-water I...I've e-ever ha- had!"

Gettie imagined her having to rely on creek and dirty river water to survive in the forest. Resnik ordered a hovercraft to transport all five of them to the hospital. He wanted Isha to meet Dr. Al. Neko once again stepped into the motherly role.

"Honey, we want Dr. Alexandria to give you a check-up. You've been living off the land for a while. The doctor can look you over just to make sure you don't have any parasites and so on."

Isha's big eyelashes fluttered a bit. Neko thought she might start crying.

"I'll go with you," offered Neko.

Isha nodded.

This time Gettie was ready! He anticipated another show of emotion from his girlfriend. Sure enough, she turned to hug him. He hugged back this time! It was system overload! His whole body experienced a ping of adrenaline! His arms went all the way around her skinny frame. He didn't want to let go but was instantly overcome with the self- awareness of everyone watching. Isha uttered a subtle vocal noise. Young love was inflamed! And just like that, the embrace was over. The rush abruptly came to an end, for both of them. Gettie's perfect white skin turned rosy once more.

Neko took Isha's hand and departed into the examining room, leaving the boys behind. "Isha, honey, it's standard procedure to put on an examination gown. You'll have to change out of the clothes you're wearing."

Dr. Al showed them a changing room. Isha was reluctant and stood still for a second.

"Do you want me to go with you?" asked Neko. Isha nodded.

She proceeded to disrobe. When she got down to just underwear, Isha slipped on the robe, then turned away from Neko to drop her panties. Her hands went over her mouth! Isha gasped loudly! Then tears began flowing profusely! Isha's body began shaking! Neko grabbed her and held on tight.

"I've got you! It's okay, honey." Isha turned to face Neko, burying her face in Neko's chest. Neko looked down at Isha's bald head and kissed it.

Dr. Al could hear crying. "Is everything okay?"

Neko opened her eyes to see the problem. The new panties had a significant spot of blood on them.

"We'll just be a sec," responded Neko. She knew at the best of times Isha had a hard time talking. This would have to be handled delicately. "Isha, do you know what a menstrual cycle is...a period?"

She shook her head no.

"Does your stomach hurt?"

"Wh-when I h-h-hugged G-Ge-Ge..."

Neko offered help. "Gettie?"

Isha nodded.

Neko had a clear picture now, and she knew Isha felt bad about the panties. Neko reached back to crack open the door; she called softly, "Al." Dr. Al came quickly. Neko whispered something to the doctor.

Upon hearing the relayed message from Dr. Al, Resnik high-tailed it to the hovercraft! He was on a mission to retrieve clean clothes.

"Honey, this is normal. It happens to me, Dr. Al, and every girl. Your body cleans itself once a month, and red fluid comes out."

"Are…are you m-mad?"

"Oh no, honey, I'm proud! This means you're stepping into womanhood! We should be celebrating!"

Isha held tighter. "I…I d-don't h-have a m-mom!"

Neko's eyes filled with tears. She put her cheek on Isha's head. "You do now!"

Neko's tears ran down Isha's bald head. Isha's heart was so full it felt like it could burst! Dr. Al was back with another pair of new panties. Neko whispered to Dr. Al again.

After receiving that second relayed message from Dr. Al, Resnik turned to the boys. "Let's go, guys. Wanna go check out that new restaurant on the second level, breakfast all day?" He realized Neko and Isha needed some mother–daughter time.

"Yeah!" Raf was glad to have Gettie to himself.

Gettie shrugged his shoulders. "Sure." However, in his heart, he was put off by leaving Isha.

Resnik had total confidence in his wife's ability to ascertain any and all pertinent information concerning Isha. He took the young men to the entrance that leads to the second level. Gettie and Raf had been forbidden from going up, until now.

"Okay, guys, it takes a little getting used to."

An opening in the floor above could barely be seen. Any gaps in the transparent floor kind of blended in. Only selected buildings and green space were not see-through. Even the small stream could be seen flowing as one looked up; it dumped out directly above the small mountain below. Resnik and the young men were positioned on the edge of downtown, close to the middle of Purgatory. There was a large circle painted on the pavement and a ladder on the edge of it that went all the way up to the second level.

"We've gotta climb that?" questioned Gettie.

"No, son, the ladder is there in case of an emergency. You stand in the circle and jump. Gravity within that area is less than everywhere else.

"Cool!"

"What if you don't jump straight?" asked Raf.

"It's like an invisible tube. It focuses your body to keep you inside it." "What if you don't jump hard enough to make it to the top?" Gettie

wanted to know.

"It will. It's supposed to discern your intentions and adjust its gravity accordingly. We're still tweaking it."

"Crazy!" Raf was first to try, as usual. He stepped inside the circle and up he went, quickly! Resnik nervously watched as Raf seemed to keep his momentum all the way up. When he got close to the second level, Resnik was cringing! Thankfully, the tech kicked in to nicely slow Raf to a gentle stop at the top. He then looked down and waved Gettie up.

Walking on a glass-ish floor took some getting used to. Then eating at the restaurant hundreds of feet above the home they've known and seeing all of it through a transparent floor was nerve-racking. Fun but unsettling, at least for a while. Confidence was building as the guys explored the upper tier. This area of Purgatory was very new and sparsely populated.

The young men gradually began imagining what it would be like living up high.

"Hey, Dad, wanna move up here?"

"I do like it. I'd have to see how your mom would feel about it."

"Let's go check out the waterfall," said Raf.

Resnik was glad Neko designed a blockade around it. The mist that came off the water drop naturally landed on the green space below, watering the grass. Makan had some input on that.

Gettie's mind kept drifting toward his new love, Isha. "How do we get down?"

"As you walk to the circle, it senses you're there and lets you down. The first time is a little scary."

"What if it fails and drops you?" asked Gettie.

"It has a tertiary backup. If that fails, each rung of that ladder has a sensor that detects fast movement. If it thinks you're moving too quickly, it deploys an airbag to catch you."

Resnik positioned himself. "I'll go first."

Resnik stepped off. He dropped at a good pace. When the bottom approached, gravity slowed him for a gentle stop. Raf was next; he experienced no problems. Gettie's stomach tickled at first when he tried, then he relaxed as he came close to the bottom.

Raf liked it. "Let's do it again!"

Resnik was quick to answer. "It's not a ride. You guys need to ask before you go up again, okay?"

They reluctantly agreed.

"Let's go check on the girls." Resnik pulled out his Purgatory cell phone. "Where are you guys?"

"Eating ice cream," texted Neko.

Resnik knew where they were. He sent Raf's mother a text. "Can you keep the boys tonight?"

"Sure," was the quick reply.

Gettie walked so fast to meet Isha it was almost like a run. Raf and Resnik had to walk fast to keep up. Both being taller than Gettie made it doable. Gettie came up behind Isha and put his hand on her shoulder. She immediately put her hand on his, lifted it, then held it. She knew it was him without looking.

He offered the greeting first. "Hi."

"Ha-hi."

"Do you two want to show Isha around Purgatory and Neom? Raf, you're in charge," said Resnik.

Once again, Raf didn't want Isha to come between him and his best friend, though he liked being the new leader. Gettie didn't really care who was the leader as long as he was with Isha.

"I'm sending Gettie home with Raf tonight. Do you think Isha will survive without him?"

"Yes, we really bonded today, and she got her first period."

"Those two kids are all *hormones* at this point," said Resnik.

"Dr. Al has agreed to meet us at the Hub tomorrow morning. She found the scar. She thinks there's a computer chip under Isha's skin," said Neko.

"What about the rest of her?"

"Physically, she's really good. Al took a DNA sample. We'll know a lot more once we get to the Pillar."

Resnik woke up the next morning on the couch. He went to check on the girls who were sleeping on his bed. Isha was snuggled up against Neko, her bald head on a pillow looking very peaceful. He took the opportunity to connect with the Spirit before starting the day. Resnik then got Leal caught up on Isha and Epygen.

"Can you meet us at the Hub in a few?"

"Of course. Give me about fifteen minutes," was Leal's reply.

By the time Resnik and the girls arrived at the Hub, Dr. Al and Leal were hard at it. Neko kneeled down before Isha.

"Honey, do you know there's a bump on the back of your head?"

Isha immediately started feeling about her head. Neko guided her hand to a spot about an inch behind Isha's right ear. Isha discovered it and shook her head no.

"We would like to put a probe on it just to identify what it might be. Is that okay?"

Isha nodded this time. Dr. Al plugged the probe into the stand-up desk then touched the bump on Isha's head with the needlelike instrument.

The Pillar instantly displayed a hologram that all could see. It showed a magnified version of the computer chip under Isha's skin. They could see the words "Made by Epygen, ID #0.665" written on it.

"That's what it looks like, honey," offered Neko.

Isha was fascinated. Leal verbally asked the Pillar what it is.

"A map of the world—GPS tracking, thought relay, Internet connection."

Leal thought for a sec. "Pillar, is it capable of more?" "Yes, however, only mapping is enabled at this time."

"I think this is a test run," said Leal. "She must have gotten away before they turned on all its functions."

Resnik had a question of his own. "Pillar, can it be removed?"

"Host information needed," was the response.

Dr. Al inserted Isha's DNA sample. The Pillar responded, "Subject will have little to no after-effects."

Leal chimed in—he knew the Pillar better than anyone. "I think we found it early enough, and the full power of it wasn't activated. Her brain isn't very reliant on it yet. She may experience a very minor feeling of loss after its removal, but that should be the extent."

"That's how she found Nebraska!" said Neko.

"And got so close to the farm," added Resnik.

Neko was about to talk to Isha. She didn't have to. Isha spoke. "Ta- ta-take ie-ie-it ow-ow-out!"

Resnik looked at Al.

"I can do it now, here. I've got my instruments with me. It's a very simple procedure."

Neko looked at Isha. Big brown eyes connected to big pale eyes. Isha nodded.

Resnik also spoke up. "Isha, sweetie, if it's okay, I'm going to try and add healing to you while Dr. Al removes that chip."

She nodded once again. Al sterilized Isha's skin, numbed it, and in less than one minute the chip was removed. A couple of minutes more and the wound was stitched and cleaned. Leal asked Dr. Al to also clean the chip. He then showed it to the Pillar, turning it so the Pillar could see all sides. The computer displayed a larger, more detailed hologram.

"Put that in a safe place, brother," said Resnik.

Isha now had a small bandage on her head.

"How are you, honey?" asked Neko.

"I feel fine," she looked happy.

"Say that again!" said Neko.

"I feel really good!"

"What?" Resnik picked her up and kissed her cheek.

Neko kneeled down to give Isha a tear-filled hug and kiss. "I'm so happy for you!"

Isha looked up. "Thank you, Mr. Clayborn!"

There was no longer any sign of stuttering.

"You're very welcome!"

"It was probably the chip that was causing the stutter," added Leal.

"I thought it was because I hadn't talked to anyone for so long," said Isha.

"That's quite a sentence you just strung together, sweetheart!" offered Resnik.

"That had better structure than most of Resnik's sentences," added Leal.

They all laughed.

Leal wasn't done. "Pillar, what can you tell us about Isha's DNA?"

"No DNA mutations."

That got the attention of all four adults.

Dr. Al spoke first: "That can't be!"

Leal was astonished. "Pillar, has this DNA been altered?"

"It is 99.9 percent likely."

Isha looked at Neko. "What does that mean?"

"Most people have several mutations in their DNA. Some think deviations increase with every generation. Someone has repaired your DNA," said Neko.

Isha's long eyelashes were fluttering.

"It's okay, honey, that's a good thing. It means you're healthy and won't have to worry about inherent sicknesses and diseases."

Resnik and Leal gave each other a concerned look. They were both thinking the same thing: *CRISPR engineering.*

Neko prompted Isha. "I might know someone who would like to hear your new dialect."

Isha responded with a very clear, "My Gettie."

Neko certainly realized Isha could be bold. *That quality must have saved her life many times over*, she thought.

"Does everyone want to get some lunch?" asked Resnik.

Dr. Al had to return to the hospital. Leal needed to get back to the condo and his wife.

Neko displayed a loving, motherly face toward Isha. "Well, angel, should we go get our two young men? I bet they're hungry."

"Yes, Miss Neko."

"I can think of two girls that are also hungry," Neko tenderly grabbed Isha's hand.

Isha held Neko's hand willingly in response.

"Isha, honey, I meant what I said. I will be your mother if you want."

"I want that very much! Can I call you Mom?"

"Yes, honey, I love you!"

Resnik looked a little nonplussed. He was now trying to understand this whole new family dynamic. "Here's your hat, sweetheart," He gently placed it on Isha's head. "Should we go get your friend… brother…Gettie." *This new family dynamic is going to be complicated*, he thought.

Before departing the Hub, Resnik gave Leal a task. "Find out everything you can about A. L. Sek!"

Leal nodded his head in agreement. He's a *digger*. Resnik knew his best friend would go to extremes to research Mr. Sek. "Thanks, cuz."

They exchanged a high handshake.

Resnik gathered up his wife and new daughter on the walk to retrieve Gettie and Raf. Resnik revisited his curiosity concerning Isha's statement about wanting to find him.

"Isha, why did you set out to find me?"

Isha sincerely replied, "To change me."

"How do you mean?"

Without missing a beat, she answered, "To change my appearance, like you did to Othneal."

Resnik was taken aback. He stopped walking in order to squat down and look at her face-to-face.

"Othneal Witt?"

"Yeah, him."

"That's not common information. How do you know about him?"

She was still very matter-of-fact about her request. "My father has a file on you and Purgatory. I saw pictures of Othneal before and after you changed him."

Resnik displayed a concerned look on his face. "It was more about restoring him than changing him." Resnik was rapidly building questions in his mind.

"You sort of had mercy on him. He tried to kill you, then you fixed him," Isha's big eyes were fixed on Resnik.

"That's really not what I normally do. And he was a good friend."

Isha continued her straightforward inquisition. "Am I your friend?"

"Sweety, you're more than a friend. You remind me of someone I love very much," he glanced up at his beloved Neko. She had admiration written all over her face.

"Do you mean Gettie?" she asked.

"No, someone else"—he grabbed Neko's hand—"though I also love Gettie very much!"

"My father is evil, I know it! I needed to get away before he did more experiments on me. Can you change the way I look so he'll leave me alone?"

To Resnik, that request seemed overly simplistic for such a complicated problem. "Let me think about it." He attempted to redirect the conversation. "What a crazy day! I'm astonished at you! You are amazing! Your mom and I are so proud of you! We will always love you! I know the Spirit brought us together!" Resnik pulled Isha close and hugged her, then tilted back her hat to kiss her forehead.

"Let's get our young men, and I'll show you my favorite restaurant."

Gettie and Raf came down from Hera's condo to meet the others. Isha went up to Gettie to hold both his hands with hers. "Notice anything different?"

"Wha—" He was stunned!

"I can talk!" she was smiling broadly. "Wow," he just looked shocked. "How do I sound?"

"Good, but better."

Isha couldn't help herself; she hugged him. "I missed you," was whispered in his ear.

Once again, Gettie's emotions were thrown into turmoil! His senses were overwhelmed by her newly acquired smooth voice. This time he purposely became more aware of the way she smelled, felt, and sounded close-up. There's no way he could let go of her this time. Neko came to the rescue. She attempted to add structure to this wild girl.

"Isha, honey, we better get going, everyone is hungry!"

"Okay, Mom." With Neko's help, Isha released him.

Gettie was now in shock emotionally and mentally. And hearing Isha call his mother, "Mom" added to his incredulity. He looked to his Dad for an answer. Resnik simply gave a nod of assurance. "I'll explain later, son."

*****

The sound of water flowing over rocks the next morning woke Resnik. The little gray house was filling up fast with people. He walked down the stairs of the house that mimicked the one he grew up in. The usual suspects had taken their places once again. Isha on the couch, Gettie on the floor, and Raf in a recliner. Resnik had come up with a plan overnight to address Isha's request. First, an early morning text to Leal:

"R u up?"

"r u kidding?" Leal was always up before Resnik.

"Anything?"

"Yeah, nothing good! Everything he touches turns to evil. Epygen wants to rule the world!"

"Thx!" was Resnik's last text.

That last text from Leal reaffirmed Resnik's new plan.

*****

A cup of coffee was brought to Neko.

"Good morning, honey. I think I know what to do. After everyone gets up and uses the bathroom, we should have a family meeting."

Resnik was now resolute. A confidence had manifested in his mind. It was just a matter of time until the culmination of his plan. He waited for the kids to wake up and become alert.

*****

When everyone had been seated, Resnik began. "Isha has made a very special request. She's traveled a long distance for a chance at a better life, a new life. She's suffered greatly in her efforts to arrive here. I've gotten to know her, and I've looked at the facts. I think the time is ripe for a change. I'm going to attempt to adjust her DNA. I've done it before to restore someone. This time it will be to alter Isha's appearance."

He now looked directly at her. "Sweety, I can't give you new DNA. I'm going to try and spark recessive genes that, if given the chance, might take over. Like brown hair could go black or even blond. So it will be you, just a slightly different version of you, okay?"

She was ready and willing.

"Come over to this chair." He kneeled down in front of her to place both hands on her head. Resnik's big hands covered most of it.

Isha suddenly grabbed his forearms to push his hands away. She looked very concerned, even scared. "If I become ugly, will you guys stop loving me?"

Everyone, including Raf, got up to gather around her. "Not a chance, honey!" said Neko.

"I'm with Mom!" said Gettie.

"You'll be fine," said Raf.

They stayed surrounding Isha.

Resnik began again. He put his hands back on her head, closed his eyes, and began speaking in hushed tones. Neko had seen him heal before and knew about how long it usually took. This method was taking longer. When Resnik finally finished, Isha looked the same.

"How do I look?"

Everyone was expressionless.

She also sounded the same. Isha immediately got up to look in the mirror. No changes could be identified. She came back to Resnik.

"It didn't work," her eyes were starting to redden.

"Sweetheart, it will take time. The changes will slowly take over. And you're also going through puberty. Many more changes are on the way. If you want to go incognito, this will become the perfect time to do it."

Resnik paused for a second. "Something else came to me last night. For all this to work, you'll need a new name." He had the utmost attention of everyone in the room. "Kaylee Clayborn. Leal's working on a social security number as I speak."

They all looked at Isha for her reaction. Gettie couldn't wait any longer. "What do you think, Isha?"

"Don't call me Isha, I'm Kaylee!"

Vocal cheers came from everyone. Kaylee sat back down, physically and emotionally exhausted.

"Please sit with me, Gettie."

He squeezed into the recliner next to her. Kaylee put her head on his shoulder and passed out. Neko shot a worried look at Resnik.

"It's okay, she'll be fine. It's working!"

Independence

Brilliant red hair unfurled as she began running away. She was every bit as fast as when she was younger. Fear was dancing in her mind! He was in hot pursuit! The gap between them was closing. There was nowhere to hide in this open space. Getting caught was not an option. The only way out was up. She was now seconds away from escape! Her pursuer's footsteps were right behind her; she could hear them, even feel them. The rush of the chase was exhilarating, adrenaline kicked in! The circle was just a few more steps. The last great effort became a leap. As her feet landed, she was catapulted upward! A finger touched her heel, but she escaped! Her chaser had to settle for disappointment.

Raf was waiting on the second level. He called down, "Hurry up, I'm hungry!" His hand offered assistance to the out-of-breath seventeen- year-old girl.

"Look out, I'm right behind you!" A loud masculine voice called upward. Gettie arrived just in time to grab his prey around the waist. "You're getting slower!"

A rich, deep feminine sound uttered, "You're getting faster!" Kaylee spoke again. "It's my birthday!"

"It's my birthday!" said Gettie.

"It's actually *my* birthday!" said Raf in a strong, low, and commanding voice.

Truth was, it was birthday week for all three. Raf and Gettie were both in the hospital together after birth. They were born within hours of each other. Leal more-or-less assigned a date of birth for Kaylee. Records of her existence were few and far between, even when she was known as Isha. Dr. Al helped in determining a correct birthday for Kaylee based on physical developments and DNA evaluations from the Pillar. It was determined that Kaylee's age coincided with the boys.

"Let me go! Mom and Dad are waiting for us." Kaylee peeled off Gettie's hand from her stomach to hold it while pulling him along. Raf's long strides kept him in the lead.

Resnik and Neko saw the kids coming. They stood up for birthday hugs and kisses. Resnik was no longer the tallest man in the family.

"Happy birthday, son!" Resnik's head came to the bottom of Raf's chin. "Did I just feel some whiskers?"

Raf felt his chin with his hand. "Oh yeah, they're actually coming in, black," he was proud to say. The white hair on his head was often mistaken for gray. People often assumed he is much older than his teens. Raf decided to keep his hair very short and inconspicuous. Raf was so happy to realize his facial hair is much darker.

"Nice, you look good! I'm very proud of you!" said Resnik.

Neko also hugged Raf. "I can't believe how tall you are! Happy birthday!"

Kaylee came bouncing into the restaurant. "Hi, Mom! Hi, Dad!" She proceeded to hug both of them. Resnik kissed her forehead; Neko kissed her cheek.

Neko now looked Kaylee eye to eye at a standing height. Kaylee's hair was cascading everywhere. It's the color of new raspberries. Much redder than the average orangey shade that most people with red hair possess. Neko grasped fistfuls of it and moved it back to reveal Kaylee's intense indigo-blue eyes. A face full of freckles also came to light. "You're so beautiful, I'm proud to be your mother!"

Kaylee smiled, still holding Gettie's hand. "I'm here too, Mom." He was smiling in a facetious manner, trying not to feel neglected.

"I know. Happy birthday!" She gave him a hug then spread her arms wide to grab his shoulders. Neko lifted herself up on the balls of her feet to kiss her son on his cheek.

Resnik shook Gettie's free hand while his wife was embracing her son. "Happy birthday, son!" He winked as he looked slightly upward into Gettie's eyes. "Mothers and daughters," he said as he shrugged his shoulders.

They all sat down around a high circular table. A very special three- sided cake was on display. Resnik offered one of his premeal salutations.

"You three turn eighteen this week! On Earth and Purgatory, that's the legal age. Earth's morality is slipping. Here on the city, we hold a much higher standard of living for those of any age. Our dignity and character need to be above what we know to be on our home planet. You three have made us proud. Purgatory has a condo for each of you! Just tell me what level you want to live on. That's your present from your mother and me. Of course, you're welcome home any time. Please remember all we've tried to teach you!" He reached for Neko's hand. "Our hearts go with you! We love all three of you!"

The cake had their three names on it. Each child's name was on one plane of the triangle. Six candles were on every side. When dinner was over and pieces were cut, they discovered it was a three-layer cake. One layer vanilla, the other red velvet, and the final was chocolate.

"Raf, your mother has a special birthday evening planned. She wanted me to tell you she has a special surprise after we were done here."

*****

Thoughts and emotions began coming to Raf as he left the second level to meet his mother. He loved the family he just left, but he didn't look like any of them. *And why am I so tall?* He had been asking himself this question as he surpassed 6'1", then 6'3", then 6'6", and onward. Was he going to keep growing? Wonderings of his biological father wouldn't go away. He would once again ask his mother when he saw her. She was always vague. *I'll press her harder this time*, he thought. *After all, it's my birthday! I should know who my real father is on my special day. That would be the greatest present of all!*

He began speculating as to what Hera had planned. Like Resnik, she'd tried to be a good parent. Her method of parenting was more in the way of warnings, rather than example. Resnik was a great person to emulate. Raf remembered many good life lessons he had learned from his surrogate father. Withal, he will have to be his own man now.

"Hi, Mom."

Hera rushed to the door. "Hi, baby! Happy birthday!" She hugged her tall young man.

Hera still had her garden-gear work clothes on. Raf smelled the scent of Neom on his mother.

"I've got two presents for you. We have to go into Neom to show you one of them."

On the walk over to the Garden of Neom, Hera mentioned the condo present. "Resnik and I pulled together for that—him more than me." She grabbed one of his big muscular arms while they walked. "Do you and Gettie still go to the gym?"

"Yes, we want to stay strong for when we go to Earth. Plus, Resnik kind of requires it. Mom, tell me more about my father. Tell me everything!" His deep-throated voice was adamant.

"Okay, son. It won't be easy to hear. Are you sure you want the whole story?"

"Yes, Mom!" His voice thundered. Raf realized how excited he was. He brought it down a notch. "I've always wanted the whole story, please tell me."

Hera gathered herself together like never before. "Your father was part of a forsaken line of people, a sect. They were on Earth for a time. They were originally from the cosmos.

In fact, their task was to oversee people, humans. They were called the Watchers. Your father and others mated with human women on Earth. Their offspring were called Nephilim."

"Wait a minute! Are you saying I'm descended from a space creature? What were you doing hanging out with some interstellar being?"

"It wasn't by choice! We knew them as Dark Matter. They began attacking us in Guardian tubes. Three of us were taken to their planet."

Raf got ahead of her. "Whoa…whoa! Are you now saying one of them attacked you and that's how you got pregnant?"

Hera looked at Raf with tears in her eyes.

Raf could see her crying. He was speechless. He and his mother stopped walking. He remorsefully thought for a second. "I'm sorry that happened to you. So do they look like humans?"

"They can transform into humans. Your father's name was Azazel. I think he was maybe like a Guardian at one time, sort of magical and full of knowledge."

"You're saying he was beautiful?"

"No, not when I saw him. That's why I'm so glad you are so handsome!"

"So when you last saw him, what did he look like?" "You don't want to know."

"*Mom!*" Raf's demeanor became charged.

Hera once again had to push herself to answer her son. "Like a dragon-man."

The evening was over at that point. The second present would have to wait. Raf turned around and started walking, leaving his mother alone. Hera was now in Neom, her favorite place/her comfort zone. Withal, not even the sound of newly hatched birds chirping could console her. She questioned herself for giving in to her son and sharing so much. Hera walked to the tree she planted for Raf, his second birthday present. Sprinkles began hitting her head. She looked up, a substantial cloud hovered above. Rain started increasing. Hera sat down, getting soaked, her tears were indistinguishable from the raindrops falling inside the dome of Neom.

*****

Gettie was reminded of a talk his dad gave him when he and Kaylee were twelve, as young love had vexed the two of them. "Son, I know what you're feeling. It's a powerful, natural phenomenon that occurs between a boy and girl! In your case, it's happening while you and Kaylee are very young. You need to take it slow! There's no way the connection you guys have should be fulfilled now. You two are not going to get married soon, nor should you act like it. And remember, she's like your sister now. When I was your age, I didn't have a dad around. Life was a free-for-all. There was no structure, and no one cared. *You* have a wonderful mom who loves you and Kaylee. I know neither you nor Kaylee would ever want to disappoint her. In my experience, there's only one way to capture all these amazing desires and emotions and put them on hold until you get married."

"What's that, Dad?"

"The Spirit."

Gettie remembered that conversation like it was yesterday. Every day since, he has relied on the Spirit to give him strength to endure. Now he was eighteen, and with more independence than ever. Gettie felt he was now ready for new challenges that may come his way.

Kaylee was not ready to leave the security and companionship of living with her newfound mom and dad. Having her own condo sounded exciting but scary. A brief flash of living alone in that forest came over her mind. She knew that wasn't going to happen. Nonetheless, she became frightened. *Where's my Gettie?* flooded into Kaylee's emotions. She looked up, he was on his way down to the lower level, motioning her to step aside.

"You okay?" He could see she had a zoned-out look on her face.

"Hold me!" she put her arms around Gettie.

Her hair was in his face; it smelled like strawberries and cream.

"What's up?" Gettie knew Kaylee well by now. The little girl in the forest would occasionally reappear. She always needed someone tangible when that feeling came over her.

"*Alone*…at my own condo!" she said in a somewhat fearful manner.

"Dad didn't mean you *have to* immediately move away. We can ease into it if you want, anyway. We could live together in one condo."

"Okay." Her mouth was up against his ear; her breath tickled Gettie. "You smell good," she said as her words tickled his ear even more.

Kaylee still spoke her emotions. Usually, if she felt it, she said it.

"It's cologne, I thought I'd put some on today. Do you like it?"

She kissed his neck.

"Don't!"

"Why?"

"Mom and Dad can see us from the second level. Besides, I have a hard enough time controlling myself around you."

"I don't want to stop. I love you more than when you found me in the forest."

"Me too." He tried to change the subject. "Should we pick condos on the upper or lower level?"

Kaylee leaned back and shook her head to move hair out of her face. "How about in the same building as Mom and Dad?"

"No way! We're independent now!"

Energy

Nearly twenty years of working for Sheik Khalil were coming to a close. His age was bringing an end to his rule and his life. Prince Qusay had waited much longer than he expected to implement his own way of doing things. In his dark heart, he still blamed Resnik for the delay in his succession. The healing Resnik brought to Khalil those many years ago manifested into frustration for Qusay, not thankfulness.

Neko was expecting to say farewell to the beloved horse, Kurokaze, and to her employment on Earth. Qusay had other ideas altogether. He never lost interest in Neko. At this point, his desire for Neko wasn't for her heart; it was for her brain. She has come closer than anyone to having the ability to define energy. Neko is close to actually describing what it is. She understands it better than anyone. She's acquired many patents while working with energy. The House of Princes has benefited greatly because of Neko's genius, as has Purgatory.

"She's getting close."

"How close?"

"Real close," answered Qusay.

"Once your father dies, how are you going to keep her around?" asked Mr. Sek.

"I have a plan," said a confident Qusay.

"I heard she won't stay on Earth after your father is gone," inquired Sek.

"She doesn't have to. Trust me! Mrs. Clayborn will be glad to continue her work," Qusay displayed his usual overconfident demeanor.

For the time being, Sek reluctantly gave into Qusay, concerning Neko. "What about the other girl?"

"It's not her." Qusay had an "I don't care" look on his face.

"How can you be sure? She's the right age!" Sek was pleading with Qusay.

"She doesn't fit your description. This girl has red hair, really red hair. And freckles, lots of freckles."

"You said she has blue eyes," indicated Sek.

"Yeah, dark blue, not pale blue, like you indicated." Qusay was becoming slightly annoyed.

Mr. Sek belabored the query. "She could be wearing contact lenses?"

Qusay reluctantly went on. "Maybe. This girl is tall. You're looking for a small, skinny girl. Trust me!"

"The girl you're talking about showed up at your horse compound with the Clayborn family. She's the correct age, she has blue eyes—"

Qusay talked over him. "Listen, she's not who you're looking for! I know you have a lot invested in some lost girl. I'll keep my eyes open! If I find her, you'll be the first to know," Qusay's deep-throated, resonating voice seemed to quell Sek for now. "Besides, don't you have a guy to look into that sort of thing?"

"Yeah, he's good, I just thought since you—"

Prince Qusay cut him off again. "Listen, I've got to go. If my father's people see me here, well… you know."

He quickly touched his hand to his forehead and exited the office of A. L. Sek. His *thawb* rippled behind him like an evil cloak. Mr. Sek then called in his assistant. "William, are you still checking into the whereabouts of the girl?"

"Yes, sir, I've never stopped."

"Don't let Qusay out of your sights either. There's no telling what he'll do the very minute Sheik Khalil passes on!"

Sek's assistant also exited the office, leaving the CEO to his thoughts. *So close to serious power! Genetics, energy… then*

Purgatory itself, finally, he thought.

He could see himself having a seat at the World Economic Forum.

*****

"I'm low on energy today," said Neko as she met Resnik on the city dock. Her big eyes looked sad.

Whenever possible, Resnik would meet her upon arriving from Earth. "How is Khalil?"

"That was probably the last time we'll see each other." Her voice was soft.

"He loves you." Resnik knew this to be true.

"He told me I'm the most honorable woman he's ever known." A tear came down her face.

"You can still go down to ride Kurokaze." He tried to cheer his wife a bit.

"I don't know. Khalil told me to be leery of Qusay."

"So does that mean you're done with Saudi Arabia?"

Neko started to speak Japanese. "*Shirimasen*. I don't know. I can't think right now." She put her arm around Resnik and dropped her head on his shoulder.

"You need a neck and shoulder rub."

"Hai."

Resnik attempted to bring up her energy level. "Who are your favorite people in the universe?"

"You, Gettie, Kaylee."

"Okay, your two favorites?"

"My son and daughter." Excitement started to build; her head came up.

"They know you're coming back today. They're both coming over tonight!"

Without saying a word, Neko looked at her husband. Her emotions were now filled with vim!

The windmill next to the quaint farmhouse was turning. It is a symbol of life on the city. On Earth, not too long ago, a windmill would power a well pump to bring up water from underground. On Purgatory, the mill turns to indicate air movement that flows through the entire cube of the city. In space, air is life.

The nostalgic setting of the little gray house appealed to Neko this evening; she chose it over the condo. The sound of water cascading over river rocks soothed her as well. She couldn't help being impatient. She was anxiously waiting to see a bundle of red hair walking next to a thick shock of black hair coming over the bridge. Purgatory was just starting its dimming cycle when the two youngsters could be seen holding hands. The atmospheric walls were darkening to block solar radiation, yet the sun still reflected off of Kaylee's hair to mimic a midwestern sunset.

Neko greeted them on the front porch. Hugs and kisses were exchanged.

"Your dad's in the kitchen making snacks," Neko called. "Babe!"

Resnik came out to find a dazzling ring on Kaylee's finger. He spotted it from across the living room. He went straight for it, staring at Kaylee's left hand. "What's this?"

Upon seeing the ring herself, Neko put her hand over her mouth; she then relented. "I've never seen any gem like this. What is… Wait… Are you two…?" The woman of few words had trouble uttering any.

"Yes, Mom!" The two children spoke in unison.

Resnik put his hands on Neko's shoulders while standing behind her. "Congratulations!"

"*Omedeto!*" said Neko in Japanese. "I mean congra— I love you both!"

Resnik pretty much knew this engagement was coming. Withal, he became more interested in learning about the ring on Kaylee's finger. Even in the low light, the stone on it glowed.

Resnik reached out for Kaylee's hand. "Can I see that again? Where did you guys find it?"

"When we went to Super Earth," offered Gettie. "It sparkled, so I grabbed it."

"It's brilliant! It's like it has its own energy! Is it safe?" Resnik's eyes were glued to it as he questioned Gettie.

"Yeah, Palmer mounted it for me. He checked it for harmful radiation and stuff."

Neko also held Kaylee's hand to also get a closer look. "You deserve such a ring. You're one of a kind!"

"Dad, can you marry us? I mean, like, legally?" Gettie said apprehensively.

"Sure. We're basically living in a separate world up here. Any other world would be obligated to recognize our legal proceedings. And I've been divinely appointed to build and govern Purgatory, so yes."

"By the way, we picked out a condo together," said Kaylee.

"Together?" questioned Neko. "Are you two…slee—"

Gettie cut her off midsentence. "No, Mom, we're waiting."

Neko had respect and admiration written all over her face. Resnik chimed in. "I'm proud of you, son! I'm proud of you both!" He looked at Kaylee and smiled.

"We both wanted your blessing, Mom and Dad, and not your disappointment," Kaylee spoke her mind, as usual.

"You've got it, sweetheart! Have you told Raf about your engagement? Where is he?"

"Locked in his ivory tower," said Gettie.

Neko put two and two together. "Zouge!"

She had named it herself; the white color mimicked that of the city gates. It is currently the highest point on Purgatory.

"He's on the top floor. We chose the first floor. It's clear like most of the second level, except for the bathroom and bedroom. And if we put down a rug so no one can see…" said Kaylee.

"They get the idea, honey," offered Gettie. "We want to get married soon."

"Like this year?" asked Neko.

"Like this weekend, Mom!"

She reached back to pull Resnik's hands around her waist. She was now in her midfifties; Resnik in his early sixties. Time had become a little more fleeting. Neko was able to get her head around the idea of her favorite people not delaying their permanent bond. *Why wait any longer?* she thought. Neko turned to look up and back at her husband. Resnik loved her eyes, and he knew what that look was. He nodded.

"Okay everyone, let's eat!"

His prenuptial salutation before dinner was simple. "Congratulations, my beautiful children!"

"Hey, Dad, we're saving the condo for our honeymoon. Can we sleep outside by the river tonight?"

"By the Pishon? Sure."

After eating, the two of them relaxed by the river. Gettie had his head resting on Kaylee's lap. The sun was veiled by the city walls. The enormous moon was also partially blocked out. The distant light of Neom and the golden streets offered a soft glow. Her hair was draped all around his face, like a red curtain. Kaylee's fingers were combing through Gettie's thick black hair.

"I fell in love at first sight when I saw you in the forest!"
"You didn't even know me," said Gettie.

"You affirmed my love for you throughout that first day and every day since!"

"Every day? Even when we disagree?"

"Every day." Her head started to droop as her eyes got heavy.

Kaylee literally fell asleep sitting there while she was talking. He maneuvered himself so that Kaylee ended up with her head on his chest, her hair blanketing most of his body.

Resnik sat on the edge of the bed, about to turn out the light and lie down. With the last remaining energy of the day, Neko crawled across the bed to sit behind him. She wrapped her long legs around his torso. With her hands, she brushed his hair aside and whispered in his ear, "Make love to me. I need special time tonight."

Destiny

Resnik woke up first. His wife remained exhausted and sleeping. He peeked out the second-story window to gaze at the Pishon River, where he found Gettie and Kaylee. They were fully clothed and sleeping comfortably on the grassy shore. Even close to the water, the temperature was warm on the city. A revelation came to Resnik overnight, to have the wedding on GJ357d. Super Earth held a special place in his heart. The few times he'd visited GJ357d were all very memorable. Now his curiosity was increased by seeing Kaylee's ring. Resnik possessed a feeling…really more of an insight about exploring more of the planet Super Earth. His thoughts were manifesting into a full-blown plan. This contrivance would require the crew—the wedding party. Early morning texts were in order. The first, and least likely to be quickly returned, was to Palmer. *He may still be late-night gaming*, thought Resnik. His next text was sent to Yasti. He figured she most likely had some sort of premonition about the outing. He was correct; she immediately texted back, "I'm in." Resnik tried Leal next. "I need a wingman tomorrow. I know it's short notice."

"Gotcha covered," was Leal's response.

Resnik thought about asking one other additional person. *I'd better let Gettie do that*, he thought.

He started making coffee. Resnik suddenly remembered, "I'd better inform the happy couple about my plans." Resnik slipped out the back door to update the kids concerning his idea. As he anticipated, they were on board. He then went upstairs with fresh coffee, the kids were excitedly coming through the back-side door. Resnik looked down at his son who was a few steps below. "Please let Raf know." Gettie was off and running toward the top floor of Zouge.

Resnik knew Neko would want to hear the plans first thing. "Good morning, *akago*." He set the cup next to the bed.

"Come back to bed." Neko's eyes remained shut.

"I came up with a plan for the wedding."

"Let me guess. We're going somewhere? I did just get back from Earth!" She wasn't quite ready to launch right back into space.

"Super Earth," was his answer.

She took a sip of coffee. "Tomorrow?" Her big eyes looked through the steam emanating from the cup.

"Yes. How did you know?"

Neko held her glare.

The cell phone chimed. It was Palmer. "Yeah, I can go. I've got something to show you!" When Palmer talked like that, it was always something impressive.

"Got to go." Resnik gave Neko a good-morning kiss on her forehead.

A little adrenaline was beginning to propel Resnik along. He hopped on his personal scooter for the practically one-mile ride to the depot. A walk through the garage area saw *Derecho* docked in a corner. The Vantablack nanotube wrap had been removed. Resnik looked around; Palmer could not be seen. Mr. Clayborn continued through the depot to where *Derecho* was usually docked.

A bright candy-apple red machine was positioned in *Derecho*'s place. It was twice the size of *Derecho*. The replacement craft looked like the fuselage of a private jet on Earth. There was Palmer stepping out of it, a huge smile on his face.

"*Oh my goodness!*" Resnik was also smiling broadly. He pointed at the new vessel. "*Derecho* 2?"

"*Hayabusa*! Means 'fast wind'!"

"It does look fast!" Resnik moved close and touched it. "Is it ready?"

"I've taken it around the city. That's it so far."

"Does it have built-in weaponry and such?" Resnik walked around it searching for signs of offensive artillery.

"*Yes sir!* All the usual stuff, plus a brand-new one—a light emitter."

I'm guessing it emits something?"

"Ha. Those Guardian tubes can be really dark. I figure if we blast Dark Matter with incredibly bright light, it would work in our favor," explained Palmer.

"Genius! Let's hope we never see them again." Resnik was contemplative.

"What about that Pride thing?" asked Palmer.

"Yeah, I hope we don't see him again either." Resnik wasn't really hoping; he knew it was just a matter of time before Pride shows up again.

Resnik poked around inside *Hayabusa*. "How many people can we seat in here?"

"Room for twelve plus a bigger cargo area," answered Palmer.

"Well, let's take her on the maiden voyage tomorrow" Resnik was matter-of-fact. He trusted Palmer and the star tech enough to just get in and go the next day.

*****

"Hey, bro, I'm getting married! You're my best man!" texted Gettie.

Raf was still struggling with his emotions. He tried isolating himself in his new condo. Anger was quickly becoming his new best friend. He could count on it. Anger would even give him power at times. When he didn't like a person or a situation, depression could invade his attitude. Those feelings would often drag him down. But anger would motivate him by giving him vigor. Raf occasionally tasted hate when anger boosted his feelings. He discovered anger is like a desired addiction, an evil drug he relied on. Somehow, he liked it; he used it to deal with life.

"Hey, bro."

Gettie could tell by that simple, uninspired text that Raf would need some motivation. "We're going to Super Earth! It'll be fun! I can't get married without you! *Brothers for life*, remember?"

Raf did remember that promise from their youth. He also became intrigued about going to Super Earth. He loved visiting GJ357d in the past. Raf couldn't put his finger on why the thought of going there interested him so much. Going to Super Earth intrigued him more than his best friend getting married. In fact, he hated Kaylee coming between himself and Gettie. Raf hated it so much, he didn't want a girlfriend for himself. He viewed that choice as a way to destroy relationships.

"I remember. When are you getting married?"

"Tomorrow!"

Raf didn't have time to think it over. If he had, he might have refused to go. He focused on his desire for Super Earth and committed to be the best man.

A wedding party indeed. The crew, plus three, loaded into *Hayabusa*. Most of the crew brought at least one weapon, except Palmer who brought three. Resnik took the opportunity to offer the youngsters weapons of their own. He gathered Raf, Gettie, and Kaylee to the wall of weapons.

"I think it's time for you guys to be armed."

He started with a single-handled Disruptor. Resnik handed one to each child. Gettie was the first to ask questions.

"Hey, Dad, where's the trigger?"

"Your mind is the trigger. The disruptor is an intuitive weapon. It senses your intentions."

Kaylee added her own query. "Like when to fire it?"

Resnik clarified. "Yes, but that's just part of it. The Disruptor discerns your attitude. The weapon activates while your hand is on the handle. If you're intent on revenge, it won't fire. If you're filled with anger, it won't fire. Your choice must be for protection." He grabbed a double- handled Disruptor. "This one requires both hands on it to work. It has a bigger spread, and it's slightly more powerful. Both weapons are dependent on the user's objective for intensity of displacement. For example, if you want to kill someone or just render them unconscious, the Disruptor will sense the level of intensity you need."

Raf put his hand out as a gesture to hold the double-handled weapon. Resnik obliged. Raf looked it over. He knew using it was going to be a problem; the anger in his heart is just too strong, though he took it anyway.

Resnik showed them additional devices. "This is a Syn-app." He held a very small cigar-sized weapon. "Palmer calls it a Brain Freeze. If you touch someone or something with it, their brain function will be put on hold—and maybe shut down permanently. So be careful with it."

Kaylee instantly took one off the wall of weapons. This surprised Resnik; he didn't really expect any of them to actually choose that one. Gettie casually watched as she dropped it in her pocket.

Resnik went on, he showed the kids a bazooka-like item. "This is an Air Saver. It expels a smokescreen of aerogel. There's a weapon port at the rear of *Hayabusa* designated just for this weapon."

None of the three seemed too interested in the Air Saver. Lastly, Resnik grabbed the latest invention, the Palmer-inspired preventative device, "The Light Saver! A burst from this should blind and disorient any and all who witness it!"

Palmer was standing close, picking weapons off the wall for himself. "Light *Emitter*," he said to correct Resnik.

Resnik rephrased his statement, "Okay, Light Emitter."

Again, the three youngsters didn't show much desire for that one either. Ultimately, Raf kept the double-handled disruptor. Gettie chose the single-handled weapon. Kaylee added a single-handled disruptor and holster to go with the syn-app already in her pocket. Resnik also chose two, an Air Saver and Light Saver.

Hayabusa looked new and smelled new. It was clean and fresh; the seats were firm yet comfortable. It had an aura of speed! Even while docked, its sleek design gave the appearance of moving quickly and efficiently. The cabin was blacked out and private. The windows were adjustable so as to allow outside vision of the interior only when desired.

Resnik tried out the new copilot's seat. "Hey, it swivels!"

"Yeah, I thought you might like that. I noticed you like to check on everyone often," offered Palmer.

"Is it easy to drive?" asked Resnik.

"Yeah. To a certain extent, it's intuitive. When your hands are touching the yoke, the ship reacts to go slower or faster, just by thinking to it."

"Nice! Is the shell strong? Does it have defensive capabilities?"

Palmer began easing *Hayabusa* out of the depot's white gate. "Its hull is stronger than *Derecho*, and if I set it in defensive mode and someone or something touches it, they'll get a brain freeze."

"Like the Syn-app?"

"Kind of, but not as extreme," Palmer answered while not removing his eyes from the instrument panel.

"It would leave them dazed and confused?" Resnik remembered what Palmer's standard Syn-app had done to him in the hands of Othneal.

"Pretty much," Palmer continued. "And it connects to the energy of a tube more efficiently than *Derecho* did."

"As in quicker?" Asked Resnik.

"Yeah, it's almost instant. We're actually in now," said Palmer as they seamlessly entered the portal of Burrow.

"Is it faster in a tube than *Derecho*?" Asked Resnik.

"We're about to find out!"

Resnik swiveled his chair for a quick glance at the six passengers. Neko was looking out a window, anticipating planets going by. What he could see of Kaylee's eyes were closed. Her hair was draped over her face and Gettie's shoulder, chest, and arm. All other eyes were on Resnik. The new instrument display clearly showed their speed: 0.5 the speed of light…0.8 the speed of light…light speed…0.6 *past* the speed of light! Leal tightened his seatbelt.

"It's just hitting its stride," said Palmer.

GJ357d was already coming into view. Resnik had made a plan to meet with a Mighty One who is the Guardian of Super Earth. No need for a lighted atmospheric tunnel; GJ357d is well lit with gravity and oxygen. He felt it was now time to inform the other travelers. He turned the seat once again. "I'm going to meet with the Guardian here. You guys go and explore. As you know, it won't take long. I'll catch up with you guys on those flat boulders by that lake. We still don't know very much about Super Earth, so try and stay together." He knew Yasti would stay close, and maybe Neko, though she might want to follow the kids if they trailed off.

Hayabusa came in fast, then stopped slow. Everyone found a jacket to put on. Once *Hayabusa* landed, Resnik walked about a hundred feet away from their new spacecraft. He then stood still, patiently waiting. A mimic of himself faded into the visible spectrum while stepping toward Resnik. Yasti was vigilant. She stayed close, without being too close, holsters on her hips. Kaylee also wanted to view this rare happening.

Resnik came face-to-face with the Mighty One. Just like the guardians seen on other heavenly bodies, this entity mimicked the image of Resnik. This encounter wasn't about technology for the advancement of Purgatory. This meeting was to ascertain the beings that govern Earth. He proceeded to telepathically connect to his twin. "Is there a Mighty One overseeing Earth?"

"Not like me. He has many subordinates. They are called the Fallen."

"Does he have a name?" asked Resnik.

"You have met him—Son of the Morning…Pride," stated the Guardian.

"Yes, I've seen Pride. Can the Fallen also be seen?"

"The Fallen don't reveal their true form. Though they can manipulate their appearance to look like humans, mostly they are influencers that attempt to manipulate the minds and emotions of people."

"Like Dark Matter…the Watchers!" offered Resnik.

"Correct."

"Yasti and I both saw a Messenger on Earth! Are there many more?"

"Countless. You two were chosen. It is extremely rare to view a
Messenger."

Resnik inquired further, "Are Guardians and Messengers the same?"

"We are similar. Messengers are held to Earth only. We Guardians are held to the domain of the heavens. In their true form, Messengers have more wings than Guardians."

"Okay, so—"

The Guardian spoke over Resnik, "The Spirit will be your guide!"

And that was it. The Guardian walked away. Kaylee stared at every step he took, to the point of watching him fade out of the visual dimension. She was standing directly behind Gettie with her arms around him, hands on his chest, looking over his shoulder. "Wow, that was amazing!"

Gettie also commented, "Yeah, it's pretty cool."

Resnik now had a more complete picture in his mind of Pride and who he is. "That's why there's so much evil in the world," he said to himself. "Sometimes when I'm confronting people, I'm dealing with an underlying influence."

Neko came over to check on him. "Did you get what you needed?"

"Not as much as I would have liked. Is everyone gone to explore?"

"Everyone except your bodyguard." Neko could feel Yasti's yellow eyes locked on to her husband.

Resnik motioned Yasti to come closer. "Thank you, Miss Charmin. Would you like to look around and such?"

She got the idea. "Yeah, I'll just check out the place, if you're going to be okay?"

"It's a well-guarded planet. Enjoy yourself."

Yasti had to put effort into breaking away from what she deemed her duty. Not that she wasn't emotionally pulled toward this amazing planet. Yasti grew up in a crowded country on Earth. Desirable open land was at a minimum, and excessive people were at a maximum. Her heart longed for something different. She imagined a place less populated and cleaner. Insects reminded her of the people in India, countless and always scurrying about. Arthropods were strong, defensive, and sometimes lethal. Yasti had to be all three in the neighborhood she lived in. The only solace she could count on in the sea of chaos was the Spirit. When the Messenger appeared to her, Yasti found it natural to commit to a life on Purgatory. She took the advice from the man who saved her life and relaxed into Super Earth. Her weapons were still at her sides, nonetheless. Yasti set out looking for insects native to this planet.

"Do we know where everyone is?" asked Resnik.

"I can see Palmer. I can't see Raf," answered Neko as she looked around.

Resnik inquired of Gettie, "Hey, son, have you seen Raf?"

"How can you not see him? You know, tall...black...cotton top," said Gettie in a brotherly, humorous manner.

Resnik yelled, "Palmer, have you seen Raf?"

Palmer was actually following Raf. He yelled back while pointing ahead, "Yeah!"

Resnik, Neko, Gettie, and Kaylee moved in that direction. Leal and Yasti joined in.

Raf was onto something. As the others began closing in on him, it became clear that Raf was intently focused on something. His big frame would bend over as he picked things off the ground. He mulled over those items in his hands, turning them to examine closely, lifting them to his eyes. He would take a few more steps to find additional curiosities. Palmer was closest to Raf, gathering some of those discarded pieces to examine them himself. Once the others caught up, they realized it was rocks that warranted all the attention. Raf called them gems. They were all similar to the stone in Kaylee's ring. Each one being a different color while maintaining a certain rare glowing quality. Everyone wanted to hold one. Raf held several specific gems in his large hand.

"Check this out," he placed the gems in an exact pattern. One of them floated, sort of hovering above the others, staying stationary in the air.

"Magnets!" said Gettie.

"No," said Palmer. "I checked out the one on Kaylee's ring. It's not magnetic. I think they possess quantum energy sealed inside a hardened shell. I've heard an old wives' tale about something like them. They called the gems *nuclear diamonds*."

Palmer tried to repeat what Raf did with other gems. He couldn't make it work.

"You have to figure it out. They need to be in a certain order," offered Raf.

Now everyone tried making it work. It was to no avail. It seemed to the others there was no rhyme or reason to manipulating the stones.

"That's amazing, son! You seem to have a natural gift," Resnik was in awe.

"Yeah," Raf's troublesome emotions started to ease a bit. He was really connecting to something. He could really understand these gems, like he had inherent knowledge. Raf initially planned on hunting when he arrived, but finding these gems excited him more. He realized a sense of destiny while being on Super Earth.

"All right, everyone, we've got a wedding to do! We'll hang out a little longer after the nuptials, but for now let's gather up." Resnik began mentally preparing for the wedding. He made his way to the huge flat boulders.

This ceremony won't be about pomp and circumstance. The high point of the wedding is coming to this extraordinary planet. The reception will be back on Purgatory. Resnik took his place. Leal set up behind everyone to guard against potential party crashers. It was like an old-fashioned Western shotgun wedding, with most everyone sporting guns.

The simple wedding didn't last long. Resnik, being the father of the bride and the master of ceremony, shortened it further. After briefly administering the vows, Resnik declared the bond between Gettie and Kaylee was now legal. Everyone was given one hour before loading back in *Hayabusa*. Kaylee and Gettie made a beeline to the semblance of a cave they explored earlier. Raf went to explore for more gemstones. Yasti also committed to looking around while Leal was on duty. Palmer made his way to *Hayabusa* to dote on the new ship.

Gettie and Kaylee were on a mission to consummate their union, ASAP. The nearby and somewhat private cave would do fine. Their joining added to the powerful connection the two shared since first meeting in the forest nearly six years previously. They shared the afterglow as long as possible before getting dressed and back on the space vessel. The culmination of many years of patience was finally enacted. The marriage and special time had sealed their destiny.

Suspicions

"My father was a great man…" began the extremely sad email waiting for Neko when she returned from Super Earth. Her face displayed an expression of lament. Such a shock after the joy of the wedding. She knew what must come next. A flight to Earth needed to be organized. It's maybe the last time to Khalil's compound, the last time to see Kurokaze. And just maybe, the last time she would have to deal with Qusay. The thought of finally putting distance between herself and the prince gave her motivation to endure a funeral.

Resnik could tell her mood had changed from the excitement experienced on Super Earth. He suspected the death of Sheik Khalil had occurred.

"Khalil?" Resnik put his hands on Neko's shoulders.

"*Hai.*" She just sat there and stared at the laptop.

Resnik offered to help. "Want me to make plans?"

Neko nodded. "Everyone should go. He knew them all."

Resnik understood her to be talking about all three kids. He once again began the process of organizing another trip. Urging Raf to go turned out to be much less of a challenge than anticipated. He easily agreed to go back to Earth. Raf had become entranced by the gemstones from Super Earth (GJ357d). As long as he had those with him, his mood would remain stable.

Resnik wasn't sure how much longer Raf would feel comfortable in public places. Resnik didn't want to flat-out put a tape measure to Raf, though he appeared to be approaching seven feet tall. Raf was already drawing extra attention when around other people. And his white hair could be construed as a beacon. Resnik could tell Raf was starting to become a bit self-conscious even on Purgatory.

Gettie and Kaylee were very willing to attend the funeral. Khalil had always been more than nice to the two of them. Besides that, they also asked if visiting the farm could be part of the journey back to Earth.

Resnik didn't feel like he needed the crew just for a simple Earth trip, so he told Yasti not to go.

"It's no bother. There will be some potentially dangerous people attending the funeral," she said to Resnik.

He tried to reassure Yasti. "There will be a lot of important people viewing the body. I'll go unnoticed."

She became adamant. "All the more reason for me to come along!" "I'll be fine, but thank you," countered Resnik.

*****

The funeral was held in Dubai. The Clayborns plus Raf stayed at the Burj Khalifa, in three separate rooms. The rooms were all luxurious. Gettie and Kaylee were officially still on their honeymoon. They welcomed the opportunity to visit the United Arab Emirates. Once there, the desire to travel to Nebraska greatly diminished. Their room in the Burj Khalifa rivaled the new condo, Zouge, back on Purgatory.

"How do you like it?" asked Gettie.

Kaylee was looking out the window with her hands on the glass. "I can see the endless ocean from here."

"It's so different from looking into space while on Purgatory," said Gettie.

She turned to look over her shoulder to make eye contact. He could barely make out Kaylee's eyes hidden within a veil of unruly red hair, though Gettie knew what that look meant. He moved close to put his arms around her tiny waist, one hand on her stomach, one hand below it.

111

"The water is vast and seems two-dimensional, empty," she said in a contemplative manner.

"There's a lot of fish and life in it," offered Gettie.

"I can't see them. On the city, everything floating around Purgatory is so close I can almost grab it. Even Earth looks close enough to touch."

She took her hands off the window to direct the blanket of hair away from her neck. Kaylee's new husband took advantage of the opportunity and kissed it. She closed her eyes. "Kiss me harder, honey," she said in her rich, feminine tone.

He obliged as the honeymoon continued.

*****

Raf requested a room on the top floor. He was denied. "Those are very expensive and for very special people," he was told. Raf settled for a hotel room close to the top. Having an expansive view wasn't important, though being higher than others pleased him. Being taller than everyone in any gathering was also beginning to please him even though it was still awkward. The feeling empowered him.

Isolation was becoming comforting as well. Ever since Kaylee came between him and Gettie, solitude became his fallback. He chose to be reclusive most of the time now.

Raf took the rocks out of his pockets. He could now get them to dance about in many different ways. They were quickly becoming an obsession. The gems looked small in his overlarge hands. The nuclear diamonds varied in size from a chicken egg dimension to a baseball. He manipulated them to levitate at different heights. He could make them roll and spin. Raf got them to change positions in his hand without touching them with his fingers. The gems were like magic to Raf. He could get lost in thought messing with the gemstones.

Knock... knock... knock. Raf quickly dumped the stones in his pockets. It was time to go.

*****

A plethora of *ghutras* and *thawbs* saturated the large conference room. Many *burqas* and *hijabs* could also be seen. There were just too many people to accommodate a viewing within the normal funeral facility. The king-sized hotel conference room seemed to accommodate all in attendance. Resnik slipped in line with his family plus Raf to look upon the deceased. They were practically the only ones without veiled clothing. Resnik's thoughts of just blending in became empty.

Neko looked upon her employer, her old friend, one last time. Memories flooded her mind. Her first meeting with the sheik was incredibly brief. Over time they became friends, even good friends. Toward the end, he was like a father figure. Neko even felt loved by Sheik Khalil. Throughout her employment, she returned the favor by offering him her expertise. He was surely blessed during the time Neko worked for him, even to the point of Resnik healing Khalil those many years ago. She was so moved that tears started to form. Neko beckoned to the Spirit for help dealing with her loss. She then turned to her husband and expressed herself.

"I'm so thankful for you and the kids!"

Resnik offered a few words of his own. "But you still have a void in your life."

She nodded.

The funeral itself was next on the agenda. Followed by a time to mingle. An amazing array of food and refreshments was laid out. Neko was hoping to avoid Prince Qusay at this emotional gathering. Resnik was thinking the same. They both tried to keep a low profile. The children didn't really know anyone there; they stayed close. Raf planned on sitting down to eat as soon as possible, he didn't really want to be seen as the tallest one in the room.

Out of nowhere and unexpectedly, Qusay was in their faces. He had a small entourage with him. Resnik and his family all had a plate of food and a drink in their hands. They hadn't gotten to their designated table yet.

Qusay began by touching his hand to his heart, then lips, then his forehead.

He risked an extra glance in the direction of Raf. Resnik and his clan were at a loss to return the greeting, having their hands full. Resnik simply nodded. It appeared Qusay was escorted by what looked like two bodyguards. Two other men with a ravenous look in their eyes came closer. One with light skin, one with dark skin. The light- complected man spoke first. His gaze flitted back and forth from Resnik to Kaylee. The plate holding her food and drink began shaking a bit. Kaylee lowered her head slightly, allowing her hair to fall forward. She was attempting to hide her face. Fear came rushing into her emotions. It was him! He looked good, not like before. Somehow, he appeared to be more youthful.

Yet she knew it was the same person. What was she going to do? Where could she go? Where was her Gettie? He was behind her, not in front where she could melt into his broad back.

"Hello, Mr. Clayborn. I'm A. L. Sek."

Resnik was shocked! He expected Sek to be older and look fouler. "Hello, sir," said Resnik.

Sek continued his boldness. "Can you introduce your family to me?"

"Well…yes, of course." Resnik did as requested.

Gettie said, "Hello, sir." Raf did the same. At that point, the tall dark man standing next to Sek never stopped staring at Raf.

Kaylee gave an almost inaudible, "Hi."

Qusay chimed in, "We should let all of you sit down and eat. Perhaps we can talk later."

Resnik nodded in agreement. As the five men departed, Sek walked close to Kaylee. He nonchalantly put out a hand toward her. His index finger and thumb opened into a pinching configuration. In a nanosecond, Gettie dropped his plate and grabbed Sek's wrist. Gettie's face had fire in it! Kaylee quickly shook her head to move hair and see what was happening. Gettie's plate of food hit the floor! The noise disrupted the entire room! Kaylee's eyes went to her husband; she'd never seen his countenance displayed in such a way. Gettie was about to discard the drink he held in his other hand. Resnik stepped in between Sek and Kaylee to grab Gettie's hand and drink simultaneously. A second plate hit the floor along with Resnik's drink.

"It's okay, son," Resnik put his other hand on A. L. Sek's forearm. "You can let go. I got him."

All eyes were now on the two men holding Sek's arm.

Neko immediately took Kaylee's food to avoid a third plate crashing down. Resnik turned his attention to Sek.

Without missing a beat, Sek said, "I'm sorry, I saw a fly on your daughter. I was just trying to help."

Resnik contemplated the situation for a second. He used that moment while his hand was connected to Sek to ascertain AL's soul.

"You can let go now," said Sek.

Resnik released him.

Sek confidently added one more statement. "If you need anything at all, let me know. I'll have people clean up and bring food to your table. Please sit and eat." He glanced one more time at Kaylee and walked away.

Neko was still every bit as fast as her son. She had already safely put her own items down after attending to her children.

Neko was ready and willing if needed, to inflict her own style of acumen.

The newlyweds hugged. Kaylee was shaking all over.

"That's him," she said in Gettie's ear.

Gettie recognized the name A. L. Sek. "I gotcha," he tried to reassure his young wife.

"You're my Gettie!" Her eyes were closed.

"He's the asshole you described him to be," said Gettie. His face had become more relaxed.

Neko remained speechless as she observed the confrontation.

Raf couldn't help being curious. He couldn't stop dwelling on the tall dark-skinned man. *Why was he staring at me?* he thought. There was something familiar about him. *And he's even taller than me*, pondered Raf.

The Clayborn clan sat down at their designated table. No less than six servers hand-delivered the most excellent food and drinks to their table. While eating, the topic of conversation centered around A. L. Sek and his aggressive behavior.

"He was after Kaylee," said Gettie.

"I know. His intent is greed," offered Resnik.

"Do you think he recognized Kaylee?" asked Gettie.

"No, but I think he's suspicious. I believe Sek was trying to get a DNA sample."

Neko offered a thought. "Should we get a sample from him?" She was curious as to the actual paternity of her daughter.

Resnik looked his wife in the eye and lowered his focus downward toward his own hand. Her eyes followed. He held a short hair between his fingers. "I did."

Raf needed a break from the drama. The magic rocks seemed to be beckoning for his attention.

He excused himself from the table, indicating a need for a bathroom break. Once clear of the main room, Raf reached into his pockets and wrapped his large hands around his new addiction. He was standing in an empty, spacious hallway. He thought it was a good spot to be alone with his thoughts. Suddenly, another person came his way. Raf became startled, like he was caught doing something naughty on Purgatory as a child. He quickly dumped the gems back into his pockets and found his way outside. He looked for somewhere private to be alone.

Certainly no one will follow me here, Raf thought.

He indulged his habit once again. It didn't take long to become engrossed. The stones did as he desired, moving gracefully in and around his hands. Raf quickly became lost in his focus.

"I see you found them. Even learned how to master them," came a pleasant, deep voice with a distinct accent.

Raf was so surprised, he dropped the stones. Curiosity paused his anger, at least for a moment.

"Who are you?"

The tall dark-skinned man answered, "My name is Reen. I haven't witnessed anyone directing Azazel stones for a very long time."

Raf looked slightly upward toward the man; meeting someone taller than himself was a rarity for Raf. They both bent over to collect the topic of discussion, which had scattered on the grass.

Raf spoke again, "You know that word…name…*Azazel*?"

"Azazel is well known to my people. Your people call these gems *nuclear diamonds*."

Your people, pondered Raf. Once again, he was dumbfounded. "We had them tested. They're not radioactive."

"I know," said Reen. "They're sealed within a special stone-like casing. When used properly, their voltaic energy can do much more than float and spin."

Raf was now fascinated. "How do you know about Azazel and nuclear diamonds?"

"He is an ancestor to many. You must share Azazel's DNA to be able to manipulate nuclear diamonds."

Raf now became intrigued. *Is Reen a Nephilim? Are there more like me?* he thought.

Raf continued, "Why are you following me? How do you know about me?"

Reen looked at Raf very intently. "We have our sources." Reen was referring to an individual called the Prophet. He was hoping to introduce Raf to the Prophet soon. "I have an incredible opportunity for you! You're not alone, Raf. There are others like you and me. They would like to meet you."

Raf's head was spinning. He believed what Reen was saying. After all, Reen looked like he could be a brother. He suspected there might even be female descendants of the watchers. Raf couldn't refuse Reen's request. "I'll meet them."

Reen gave Raf a business card. It was similar to a credit card. "This is a GPS card. Just go where it indicates. Come tonight at eleven o'clock. It should take about seventeen minutes to walk there from Burj Khalifa."

They even know where I'm staying, thought Raf. He didn't have time to further engage with Reen. Raf hastily decided to accept the card from Reen. *I'd better get back to the funeral ASAP*, he thought.

He was unaware of how much time had passed in his absence. Raf was hoping no one would notice how long he was absent.

Upon his return, Gettie asked, "Everything okay, bro?"

"Yeah, I just stepped out for a sec to recover from the drama," Raf was trying to be cool about it.

Gettie apologized, "I'm sorry. That was a little crazy."

*****

"Did you get it?" asked a man dressed in black who possessed the cocky yet smooth characteristics of a seasoned politician.

"No, that damn kid stopped me," said A. L. Sek.

"Have someone scour the chair she sits in when they leave. Do you think it's her?"

"She looks a little different. It very well could be her." Sek's tone was almost subservient.

"We invested a fortune into her, not to mention twelve years of our time. We need her, Sek! It doesn't work without her genome!"

"I know, I'll get her!" Sek tried to exhibit a demeanor of confidence.

At ten thirty, Raf set out to find the location that held a promise of discovering his origin. He pulled out the GPS card from his pocket. He looked at it thoroughly. Once the card was brought close to Raf's eyes, it activated. The card displayed clear directions as it lit up. A pulsating indicator also showed his current position. As he moved, the card guided him like a tracking beacon, down the elevator and out to the street. The directions led Raf to a building with no apparent door. He looked around thoroughly. He could see nothing but a concrete wall in front of himself. There was no indication that a door might be there. As before, he held the card up to his face. A symbol was now glowing upon it. The lettering was a little unique. It read "Anackim" in slightly skewed lettering. Raf examined it with perlustration, turning the card in multiple directions. When upside-down, the word Anackim read Watchers! The same symbol then appeared on the wall in front of where he was standing. He brought the card close to the matching symbol. A hidden door opened! Raf entered. Excitement and adrenaline came over him! He hadn't felt this alive for longer than he could remember. He stowed the card in his pocket and walked forward through the very large hallway.

As he passed glass cases, a backlit light would turn on to illuminate artifacts. There were more nuclear diamonds, and they were of more varied sizes than he already possessed. Those in the display didn't need any additional lighting. They glowed brightly on their own. Then Raf saw some sort of metal. They could have been tools or weapons —he couldn't tell which. Primitive clothing came next. Animal skins melded with colorful fabric were displayed on extralarge mannequins. He suspected these garments to have been worn in Azazel's time. Raf moved forward. Hand-painted pictures of beautiful women lit up next. These Earth women were of all races and colors. Most of them had noticeable makeup on their faces. The end of the hall was now in sight. The last display showed star charts.

Raf then stepped through jumbo-sized theater-style doors. A room full of people was seated. As he entered, they all stood up. Raf was blown away!

There must be at least seventy-five people here, he thought.

Raf became transfixed. He wanted to pause and take it all in. His eyes swept the room. Everyone there was looking back at him. This attention was much more than random people gawking at him because of his height. He had known that discomfort. This situation was different. Raf felt they may be reciprocating the awe that he was feeling. Reen was also there; he came up to Raf and extended a hand.

"Welcome, cousin. Take your time, there's no need to be in a hurry." Raf continued scanning the room. He recognized a few athletes. The one thing everyone had in common was their size. All were large. Some displayed great height, while others are extremely big. Yet some were both. A few looked very muscular and very strong. White skin to black skin,

European to Middle Eastern and African could be identified. In Raf's world, these people didn't exist.

He was astonished and delighted to find them here.

Reen remained by his side. "They are all here to meet you."

Raf then looked at Reen with incredulity. "Why me?"

"These people are your distant relations, your cousins!" Reen was very genuine in his tone.

Raf responded, "My mom doesn't have a lot of family."

Reen answered, "Most of these individuals are descendants of Azazel, your father. A few came from Semyaza and Baraqel. We are all your family!"

Raf was overwhelmed! *Could this be true? A family? Would they embrace him as one of their own?*

Reen spoke further, "Would you like to meet them? They want to meet you."

Raf nodded. Reen motioned the front row of people to advance. Raf's eyes were immediately drawn to one individual. He'd singled her out from an earlier glance. She reminded him somewhat of his mother, but taller with much longer hair. From a distance, this girl appeared to be lighter-skinned, and the ends of her hair were goldish in color. Ten people came to Raf before her. Many hellos and "an honor to meet yous" were offered. Real nervousness kicked in when she stepped in front of Raf. A hand was extended to him.

"Hi, I'm Shinar. It's really great to meet you!" she said while smiling broadly.

"Hello," Raf managed to say, though he thought. *Your face is adorable. Can I touch your hair?*

Raf froze in time. He guessed her age to be close to his. In an instant, he knew what it was like to feel what Gettie and Kaylee must feel. Shinar stirred his heart. His struggling emotions were elevated into a place filled with light. Raf's anger was relieved by hearing her voice and seeing her smile.

However, he was in shock. All he added to his greeting was, "Nice to meet you."

Shinar moved on. Close to seventy other admirers were waiting in the wings to greet Raf. He didn't have time to dwell on Shinar—at least not now.

After the meet-and-greet, Raf contemplated the thoughts he had put on hold. He was suspicious as to why he was so highly esteemed among his distant relatives, some of which were famous. And he was more anxious to revisit his curiosity concerning Shinar.

Was she also a distant cousin? He thought. *Where does she live?*

Raf decided to express his desire to Reen, who was still in close proximity. "Sir, do you know Shinar?"

"Please call me Reen. I do know Shinar. I can set you two up with a private meeting. However, please address this audience first. They've gathered here to meet you."

Raf snapped to. "Yeah, I can do that…before I talk to Shinar."

He didn't pause to think this through. Raf had a pretty girl on his mind. "What do I say?"

"Just tell them a little about yourself. Where you live, who your parents are, stuff like that," Reen was trying to sound nonchalant. Like the others, he really wanted to know more about the Watchers, Azazel in particular.

Raf attempted to pull himself together. Public speaking wasn't his thing, though it was required in school. He nervously stepped up onto the slightly raised podium. The tall young man now appeared to be well over eight feet tall. Somehow, he liked this vantage point. Some kind of confidence kicked in. Once again, all eyes were on him.

"I'm Raf, or Rafykei. I live on Purgatory with my mom. I'm eighteen years old."

As Raf began his speech, his commanding voice became his ally. It thundered across the room without any microphone to amplify it. He could have read a grocery list, and the audience would have still been captivated.

"I studied history and politics in school, and also took some leadership classes. My mother is Hera Wombosie. She's a farmer, a horticulturist. She used to live in Africa. My father is…was Azazel from Planet TrES-2b."

With that last sentence, the crowd exuded verbal utterances of all kinds. Random questions then followed. Raf wasn't sure what he'd gotten himself into.

"So he's dead?" came a stray comment.

"How did he die?" came another.

"Who killed him?" called out someone else.

"Did you know him personally?" said another person.

Reen chimed in, "One at a time, please."

Raf tried to calmly reply, "I didn't know him personally. My mom met Azazel on the Dark Planet. I've never seen him myself."

"Did she know Baraqel?" came a cry.

"Has she seen Semyaza?" asked another.

Raf could see where this was going. "I'll try and get answers for you! Give me some time." He glanced around, looking for Reen to bring him some relief.

Reen stepped up to take over for Raf. "That's enough for now. We'll schedule another conference soon. I promise more answers for all of you. Thank you!"

Reen stepped down from the podium and made his way to Shinar. Raf watched with great interest. He became delighted as Reen motioned him to follow Shinar and himself to a secluded room. Once Shinar and Raf entered, the door was shut.

Raf once again applied good manners. "Please have a seat. Thank you for meeting me privately."

Shinar had manners of her own. "You're welcome."

Raf sat down also. He liked the sound of her voice and became curious about her accent. "Where are you from?"

"The Dominican Republic." Her brown eyes stayed fixed on his black eyes.

Shinar's pretty round face has big features, big eyes, broad nose, and substantial lips. Raf was drawn to her long curly hair. It was big and full as it framed a large circle around her face. He thought the golden-blond ends reminded him of the sun viewed from the City in Space. As Raf studied her, words could not be found.

Shinar eased his tension. "You're famous," she said in a matter-of- fact way.

He pointed to himself. Raf still didn't know what to say.

Shinar continued, "It's because of your ancestry. You descend directly from a leader of the original Watchers. You're like a pureblood."

Raf's emotions turned a corner! He'd always thought of himself as an outsider. His surrogate father, Resnik, had always treated him like a son, but the facts remained. Raf was different. His color, his height, even his hair made him stand out. He'd always thought of himself as lesser than others, and with no biological father in his life. But now his attitude was starting to soar! Raf realized it might take a while to wrap his head around the whole thing. He was willing to commit as much time as needed.

Shinar could almost feel Raf's excitement. "Listen, this has got to be a little crazy for you. Give me your GPS card, and I'll give you mine. When you exchange them like this, they will find each other. They imprint to your eyes, so they're sort of loyal to their original recipient. If you want to talk later, touch the icon on the card that indicates me."

It was getting late. Raf felt it was time to go back to the hotel. He found it extremely difficult to even think about leaving Shinar, let alone getting out of his chair and walking away. In a few short minutes, Shinar had become the most important thing in his life! Or at least she seemed that way. As long as he possessed the card, he felt he had the strength to depart from her. Raf stood and shook Shinar's hand. On this second time holding it, he noticed it was a bit bigger than his mother's. However, it was not a working hand like Hera's. Shinar's hand was soft and very feminine.

He realized this was going to be a new path to follow. He was anxious to take it. He was no longer suspicious; Raf trusted Shinar.

The Will

Arriving back on Purgatory meant isolation. Raf no longer desired to be alone. He cherished the GPS card in his pocket because it represented a connection to Shinar. Even the nuclear diamonds took a back seat to her. He and the Clayborns left Earth hastily. Raf hadn't yet tried to use the card-to-card communication. He held his card up to examine the display on the face of it. "Signal failed" was indicated. He figured it was out of range but wanted to try anyway. He would now have to wait several days until the return trip to Earth and the reading of the will. Raf wasn't even sure he was invited. A conversation with Resnik was warranted. He left the second level to locate his surrogate father. Raf found him at the Hub.

Resnik noticed the tall, bold figure of Raf walking in. "Good morning, son."

"Good morning, sir. Can I ask you something?"

Resnik could tell Raf needed some one-on-one time. "Sure, I'm just finishing up. You wanna grab a doughnut or something?"

Raf agreed. His mind was a little more settled after realizing Resnik could meet with him. They walked a few blocks to Heavenly Doughnut.

"What's on your mind, son?" began Resnik.

Raf had a demeanor unlike anything Resnik had seen before. Raf looked a bit needy and maybe apprehensive. "Can I go back down to Earth with you when they read the will?" Raf said almost shyly.

Resnik was taken aback a little. He paused for a moment. "Yeah, sure. Did you fall in love with Dubai?"

For a split second, Raf thought Resnik was going to say *a girl* instead of *Dubai*. Raf now paused. "Ah, yes." This wasn't altogether true, though he did fall in love (or maybe like) with

Shinar. Raf wasn't familiar with strong feelings for a girl. To this point, he was put off by Gettie's feelings for Kaylee. Raf had found the thought of having a girlfriend irritating. That was until meeting Shinar. Now all he wanted to do was see her again. And he wasn't quite sure about sharing his Anackim experience with Resnik, but nonetheless needed to inquire about something.

"Sir, can I ask you another question?"

Resnik realized this was going to be incredibly important to Raf. He wasn't usually so intense with his queries. "Of course," Resnik finished his doughnut and became focused on what Raf was going to say.

"Do you know who Baraqel and Semyaza are?"

Resnik was once again taken aback. He wondered when this time might come up. *But what sparked Raf's interest?*

Resnik answered directly. "Yes, I do, they were allies of Azazel."

Raf was now gaining momentum. "You mean Azazel, my father."

Resnik felt there was no turning back now. "Yes."

Raf decided to go further down this rabbit hole. "Baraqel and Semyaza were also on the Dark Planet?"

Resnik responded. "Well, yes and no. We encountered Semyaza in open space. He was killed while trying to kill me!"

"And Baraqel?" added Raf.

"He confronted us while on the Dark Planet. He was eliminated while trying to kill Palmer."

Raf was now taken aback himself. Before meeting his cousins, these names meant nothing to him. Now Semyaza and Baraqel were like uncles, or at least some sort of family. One of them could even be related to Shinar. Confusion started to commune with the anger already in Raf's mind.

Could Resnik and his friends be considered indiscriminate killers? he thought. *Were Azazel, Semyaza, and Baraqel noble beings at one point in the distant past? Did they really deserve death?* Raf's own alliances were now in question. *Was he a citizen of the sovereign Purgatory, or does he belong to an ancient people of great renown?*

Resnik could see Raf was digesting this new knowledge. He figured some of these inquiries must have been inspired by talking to Hera. Maybe all of them, he didn't know.

"Are you going to be okay, Raf?" asked Resnik.

He snapped to. "Oh…yeah, I'm fine," Raf's manners kicked in. "Thank you, sir. When do we go back down?"

"In two days. Gettie and Kaylee also want to go. They're going to the farm. You can join them if you like."

Raf once again had to mentally pull himself to the present. "Yeah, thanks for the offer, but I would rather go to Dubai. I already miss it."

Resnik hadn't planned on so many wanting to return to Earth so soon, although he was fine with it. Right now, it was time for him to make his way back to the Hub to see the results of A. L. Sek's DNA sample.

"We'll leave the day after tomorrow. You're welcome to travel along with the rest of us," Resnik gave Raf his signature smile. They parted ways so Resnik could return to the Hub.

*****

Leal had the breakdown from the DNA search. "He's been modified!"

"Okay. But what about Kaylee? Is she related?"

"Oh…yeah, not even 1 percent," said Leal with confidence.

Resnik had relief written across his face. "Well, that's good. What is Sek's modification?"

Leal was still working with the Pillar while answering his friend. "He's been made to look younger and attempts were made to make him taller."

Resnik's imagination started kicking in. He stroked his beard while contemplating this new information. "Tweaking DNA, implanting computer chips…" While Resnik was thinking, Leal chimed in, "Artificial intelligence!"

"Yeah," said Resnik. "Most likely, but definitely recombinant engineering. And trust me, I'm sure Purgatory is still in their sights."

"What do you want to do?" asked Leal.

"I think I should snoop around when I go back down in a couple of days. Wanna go with?"

"I don't think I can leave Annette now. Even with the low gravity of Purgatory, she's really struggling."

"No worries, you belong here with her."

He now expected to hear from Yasti very soon. Until then, he sought after his beloved wife. Resnik knew she would want to know the DNA results. He found her in the Hub, a couple of floors up.

Neko was engaged with the Pillar.

"Hey, honey," Resnik greeted Neko with a slight pat on her behind.

She was moving her arms in an animated way on the Pillar and in front of it. She turned to face him. "Hi, babe."

Resnik felt good about Kaylee not being related to A. L. Sek and was anxious to relate it to Neko. "I've got the results of Sek's DNA."

Neko was silent in anticipation. Her hands were now on the sides of her face.

"Kaylee is not related to him. Leal and I think she might be an experiment. It's likely she was designed in a laboratory."

Resnik could almost see gears turning in Neko's mind. "That's why they want her so badly."

Neko put her arms around her husband. She now spoke. "They can't have her! I don't care how she was conceived. I love her so much!"

"I know. I do too. When we go back down, I'll see what I can find out. Maybe there's a way to dispel Epygen's interest in Kaylee."

Neko had a tear in her eye. "She makes Gettie so happy. I'll help you any way I can."

"I know you will." Resnik put her at arm's length, then used the back of his index finger to wipe away a tear from Neko's cheek. "I think you should attend the will reading while I do some digging."

Neko gave a slight nod. Resnik knew his wife would stop whatever she was doing in order to help or even save him. She'd done it before on several occasions. Neko would also do anything to protect her children. *Hopefully, it won't come to that*, thought Resnik.

He glanced at his cellphone. Yasti had sent a text indicating her desire to come along. Resnik felt he would need her to accompany him this time. "Yes, please come along," was his return text. Yasti had telepathically received a directive from the Messenger concerning Resnik's next adventure. She was compelled concerning the risk he was about to step into.

The traveling crew was starting to shape up. It was now time to inform Wilson of the travel plans to prepare *Ornan* for the journey.

Resnik knew Palmer would most likely desire to stay on Purgatory. Earth held unwanted temptations for him. Substance abuse was his nemesis at one time. The City in Space had become a safe zone for Palmer.

This trip to Earth was shaping up to be like a journey into a tube. A Guardian-tube-like concern was building in Resnik's mind. The brevity of dealing with Epygen again began to also weigh heavily on Resnik's emotions. A few people associated with that corporation had tried to kill him in order to take over Purgatory. He felt he would need to rely heavily on the Spirit for this dangerous Earth journey. A good night's sleep will also be helpful. The comforting sound of the Pishon River flowing over rocks just outside the Purgatory farmhouse would aid in sleeping tonight.

The new day was spent in final preparation for a return to Earth and the reading of the will. During the overnight, the Spirit gave Resnik insight concerning Epygen. He also received passwords to be used if he could somehow manage to get deep inside the offices of Epygen. For now, Resnik made his way to the garden of Neom so as to walk the dome perimeter. Earth looked somewhat more special from there while soaking up the smells and sounds emanating from Neom. He even noticed a bat flying about. His eyes followed it upward. Thick clouds now became a permanent fixture above the garden. Resnik wondered when it would rain next.

He was a bit somber gazing down at his home planet. He now viewed Purgatory as his full-time home. Earth has changed so much in the last twenty years. The advancement of technology was magnificent. Electronic devices of all kinds allowed every sort of convenience. Almost everyone was incredibly reliant on the Internet and cell phones.

Maybe too reliant, thought Resnik. *And what about constant rumors of wars and armies invading other countries? Shouldn't we be more civil to one another?*

A subtle fear was building in his mind concerning his trip the next morning. Going to the farm in the heart of the country was one thing, entering Silicon Valley to invade Epygen would be altogether different. Resnik felt good about Neko arriving half a world away in Saudi Arabia, hopefully out of harm's way—although he knew he could use her help in California.

Yasti will most likely be sufficient protection, thought Resnik.

*****

"Are you sure you want to go back? It would be like returning to the scene of the crime," asked Gettie.

Kaylee answered with fervor, "I think I need to. I feel like it would free my emotions a little. When memories haunt me, I get scared and afraid. If we go together, I might be able to conquer my fears."

"Okay, but we're staying at the farmhouse. We're not sleeping in that nasty tree or under the railroad bridge," said Gettie while snickering.

"And this time we can sleep together—and in a real bed instead of the couch." She gave him a smooch.

Bright and early was the new Purgatory morning. *Ornan* was charged and ready. Wilson and his easy-going demeanor were waiting in the pilot's chair. His friendship with Resnik went way back, almost as long as Leal's relationship with Resnik.

"What happens when you get eaten by an elephant? You run around and around in his stomach until you get pooped out," was one of Wilson's many corny jokes. Besides his cheesy one-liners, he was the funniest man Resnik had ever known and his second best friend. Wilson was a counselor before his retirement and subsequent move to Purgatory. Piloting *Ornan* suited him. The lower gravity of the City in Space, along with being able to sit down while working, allowed him to excel at his job. Everyone traveling in *Ornan* got a sample of Wilson's humor along with his kind personality. He even bent an ear and offered comfort to those

132

who were nervous fliers. Wilson was an easy recruit for both piloting *Ornan* and living within Purgatory.

"Sup, old friend," said Resnik as he entered *Ornan*.

"Sup," responded Wilson.

Resnik was dressed to blend in with the California tech crowd—blue pants, brown shoes, a nice shirt, and sports jacket; no tie. Neko wore a very elegant, flowing black suit, appropriate for the reading of the will. Her black hair blended perfectly with her clothes. Raf was wearing nice clothes. His white hair was cut extremely short. His face displayed the slightest hint of a beard shadow. He may have even applied some cologne.

"Who smells good in here?" asked Gettie. Raf ignored him.

Gettie and Kaylee donned hiking gear. Yasti had on loose-fitting casual clothes so as to hide many weapons underneath her garments.

The passengers prepared for the ninety-minute journey to Earth.

Ornan orients to a vertical axis when landing at its charging dock on Earth. It then tilts forward to allow the passengers to disembark. After this occurred, Gettie and Kaylee boarded a plane to Nebraska. Neko and Raf left for Saudi Arabia. Resnik and Yasti stayed in California to infiltrate Epygen. Wilson departed soon after their space shuttle recharged. All were on their own mission. The three couples set out with a strong will to succeed, the Spirit as their ally.

Resnik and Yasti decided to pose as an investor with his legal attaché. Resnik had cut his hair and beard to go incognito. Yasti wore glasses to slightly disguise her animallike yellow eyes. They took an Uber for the short trip from the dock to Epygen. The two exited their driver's Tesla and began walking toward the building that displayed an enormous emblem: "Epygen: Unlocking the Future."

Resnik suddenly remembered his last conversation with a Guardian: "There are countless Messengers." He needed one now. He and Yasti stopped before entering the beautiful glass-sheathed building. Within his thoughts, Resnik connected with the Spirit to request help from a Messenger. Within seconds, a tunnel-like vision appeared in Resnik's mind showing him a path. It led through the front doors and brought them to a specific security guard. Resnik knew it was a messenger, though he looked like any of the other uniformed guards. Without exchanging words, the three walked together down hallways and up an elevator. A door was shown to them a short distance from the elevator threshold. Resnik looked down and tried turning the knob. It was unlocked. He glanced behind before opening the door. The Messenger was gone!

The elevator door was still open, and no one could be seen besides Yasti and himself.

"I guess this is it," reasoned Resnik.

He and Yasti went through the unlabeled door. A great surprise awaited them! Lights went on. Neither Resnik nor Yasti had ever seen such a large office. An oversized computer monitor came to life and lit up. They hastily moved toward it. He put his hands on the keyboard. The computer said, "Good morning, Mr. Sek."

*****

Gettie and Kaylee were approaching the small Fourth-of-July City in the heart of Nebraska, named for its elaborate Independence Day celebrations. From overhead, as the small electric airplane descended for a landing, they saw the farm fields and circle formations of pivot irrigation. They had transferred from the large jet they boarded in California to a multiprop E airplane twenty miles from the small country airport. They were less than a mile from the farm. Opting not to drive, they chose to walk on the gravel road and across the railroad tracks. The electric Rivian pickup awaited in the barn if needed.

Gettie was holding his wife's hand while walking past the giant cottonwood trees. "I've never been here without Dad and Mom. It feels kinda weird," he said.

"Yeah, I know what you mean," offered Kaylee. She grabbed one of his hands with both of hers, then faced him, her hair bouncing all around her face. "Let's take a nap before we go hiking."

Gettie knew this was a euphemism for special time. He couldn't refuse the special physical connection with his wife. They entered the farmhouse and went straight to a bedroom. The stronger gravity offered a slightly different dimension to their special time together. When they were finished, Kaylee fell asleep quickly, followed closely by Gettie.

"Are you ready to go?" said a very awake Kaylee.

"A… Yeah…give me a minute," said Gettie. He was trying to shake the sleep from himself, knowing the hike might become stressful. Kaylee would often get overwhelmed when a stray thought about being alone in the forest entered her mind.

Maybe it will be like she said, a release of her fears by facing them, he thought. *Time to find out*. He shook off sleep and got out of bed.

They got dressed in their hiking clothes and began to retrace Kaylee's journey back to when she was Isha. The forest was in full bloom this time, making the hike a bit more challenging. Most of the trails were obscured by overgrown foliage. They passed a hawthorn tree that displayed three-inch-long needlelike spikes, giving it a wide berth.

"Was that here before?" asked Gettie.

Kaylee simply shrugged her shoulders. Everything seemed more menacing than before. They decided to make their way to the railroad bridge first. Though getting there was not easy due to tall, thick native grasses and a few fallen trees, Kaylee knew she was on the right path as she could feel emotions coming to the surface.

She motioned to her husband, "Go left here."

The railroad tracks were now in view. They could even see some sort of train-like apparatus coming down the tracks toward them. Slipping under the bridge, Kaylee went straight for one of her dugouts. She cautiously peered into it, anticipating seeing items she might have left there. Sure enough, there was one of her sharpened sticks and some discarded bones.

Wow! I eat so well now, she thought.

Deciding to crawl into the dirt hole, she got on her hands and knees. Much taller now, the crevice was a tight fit. She squeezed in and looked up at Gettie.

You look like a whole different person, said Gettie, remembering the dirty face and matted hair of Isha.

Kaylee had become beautiful! Her once-nasty brown hair was now a huge blossom of brilliant red. Her picturesque face now possessed freckles on white skin. Kaylee's slim, shapely frame was that of a woman, not a skinny little girl. And her heart was now full of love.

She had a family who loved her, and she loved them. Her days of being abused and used for experiments seemed in the distant past.

"Should we check out the tree?" asked Gettie.

Kaylee crawled out of the hole to grab her husband's hand. "This way."

She led them onto the overgrown path. Foliage brushed their legs and hips as they pushed through the thick greenery. Gettie remembered tracking Isha when the path was clearer. This time, he was relying on Kaylee to find her one-time home in the hollow of an old tree. She slowed as they approached it. The hollow stump was still intact, though a bit more weathered. The upper section of the tree was totally disconnected now and had completely fallen into the river. Part of it was above the surface of the water, collecting debris that floated along the surface.

The two of them stared at each other, waiting to see who would volunteer to look inside first. Gettie stepped forward. He was now tall enough to peer in without elevating himself. He saw something that intrigued him—a corner of a piece of paper barely visible. He decided to climb in to get a better look. Gettie's feet landed on dried-out bones and sticks. He dug around in the detritus to uncover the photograph. He couldn't help but stare at it for a while. He flipped it over. It had a date on the back along with a small note. He had glimpsed this portion of it before he had gotten in the tree. He became intrigued while reading it several times. He examined both sides of the photo many times. The image on the photo was of his father, shaking hands with a man wearing a shirt that had *Epygen* embroidered on the left breast pocket. His dad looked twenty years younger.

Maybe it was taken when Purgatory was first established, thought Gettie.

The note on the back said, "Off to a great start—William." Gettie wanted to ask Kaylee how she had it in her possession.

"Hey, honey, I found something," Gettie called to his wife.

There was no response.

"Honey, can you hear me?" Gettie tried again.

Deciding to stand up and see what was the matter, with the photo still in his hand, he raised his head over the rugged rim of the stump. Kaylee wasn't there. He looked harder and in all directions. "Am I missing something?" he said to himself.

Panic started entering his emotions. He climbed out of the tree as quickly as possible. He tried to be as quiet as possible, listening intently. Only one path looked as if it had been used recently—the one he and Kaylee had come in on. Gettie took it, beginning to backtrack while running. Weeds and grass scratched his arms as he ran back to the bridge. As he got closer, he could hear an engine gearing up. Despite being tired, he attempted to sprint to where the sound was coming from. The piercing noise of high-pitched air brakes came next. Crossing the creek was the final obstacle. He splashed through it to scramble up the steep bank. Out of breath, on his hands and knees, Gettie watched the railroad vehicle they'd seen earlier moving back in the direction it had come from.

Kaylee was gone!

*****

The will was about to be opened. Qusay's greed made him very anxious in anticipation of what he might inherit. Meanwhile, Neko patiently waited, not expecting anything. Sheik Khalil had gone to extremes to ensure no one could tamper with it. His personal friend and lawyer, Muhammed, kept the will protected. Now all in attendance were about to hear the outcome.

Muhammed unfolded the legal document. "The last will and testament…" he began.

Neko was named first. She was awarded the horse, Kurokaze. Muhammed continued, "The entire horse compound located west of al Lulu, I bequeath to Neko Clayborn."

Prince Qusay was inflamed! *How could my father do such a thing?* he thought. He was outraged! He had known a lifetime of indulgence. He didn't really care about Kurokaze, but the *entire* compound? *That's too much,* he thought.

His indulgent emotions were being tested at a high level. Qusay seriously considered getting out of the chair he was sitting in to confiscate the will. It took every ounce of control he could muster to stay seated. A restraining hand on his shoulder from his assistant also helped Qusay remain in his chair.

Muhammed added even more: "I bequeath rights to Neko Clayborn for the energy research developed by Neko Clayborn at the al Lulu facility." That information alone was worth millions. That was the last straw for Prince Qusay. He gave instructions to his assistant, then left the room in a rage of frustration.

Neko sat calmly, yet she was astonished. *I don't really need anything*, she thought. She even felt a little embarrassed about being lavished upon. *Is there going to be more?* she pondered.

Muhammed spoke again. The sheik's private aircraft was now offered to Neko. *Outrageous*, she was astonished while contemplating the generosity of her former boss. *Though that item could be useful*, she reasoned in her mind.

All the endowment seemed over-the-top to Neko. She never expected such favor. Her courteous visit turned into quite a bestowment upon herself. Neko witnessed Prince Qusay leaving earlier before all of the will was read. Muhammed still wasn't finished, however. Most of the rest of Khalil's assets went to Qusay. Neko could see the prince's assistant making notes of the final items. In her mind's eye, Neko dared to be hopeful that Qusay might now lose all the unrequited affection he had held for her these past many years.

*****

The GPS card was up and running. Excitement, coupled with a dose of adrenaline, was capturing Raf's emotions. Thoughts of Shinar were filling his mind. *Not long now*, he began thinking.

Shinar had responded to his card message: "Meet me at the Dubai Mall food court."

His hands were sweaty. He even thought of putting on a *ghutra* in order to blend in. Being almost seven feet tall made him a little self- conscious. She had seen him before, but maybe he should look more normal or average. Raf wanted to make a good second impression. The first one was unplanned and took him by surprise. Having more time to think about this one made him nervous. *No time to worry about it anymore*, he thought as he walked through the entry doors of the food court.

Shinar's favorite snack was nachos. She asked Raf to meet her for chips and a smoothie.

He located the ordering counter. *Now to find Shinar*. He didn't have to put much effort into looking around; Shinar found him.

"Hey, Raf." She gave him a hug. He was relieved, surprised, and shocked all at once.

"I saw you come in," said Shinar with a large smile on her face. "Are you hungry?"

Raf was glad she opened the conversation. "Yes, very hungry."

"Let's get my favorite. Is that okay with you?"

"Sure!" He would've eaten anything she chose.

"I was so glad to see your message on the GPS card. I thought maybe you forgot about me."

Shinar's voice sounded extremely pleasant to Raf. "When I first tried it, I was out of range."

"I was hoping that was the reason for your silence," offered Shinar.

Raf reassured her further. "I tried to message you when I was on Purgatory, but I was too far away."

Shinar's round face displayed excitement. "I had... have something to tell you. The Anackim have something to offer you."

That statement captured Raf's attention. Was she speaking for the Anackim or merely giving him a heads-up? He couldn't decide.

She continued, "Can you meet with them…I mean us?"

He thought for a second, seeing Shinar was his priority, connecting with his kin would also please him greatly. He decided to comply with her request. "Sure, when do they want to get together?"

"After we eat," she said enthusiastically.

He nodded. "Okay." Raf was becoming so fascinated with Shinar that he may have agreed to anything she had to say.

They got up to order some food. Raf began to relax a bit. He put his hands in his pockets while waiting in line. He let Shinar decide what to eat. Raf wasn't always sure of the protocol of Earth restaurants. The stones were beckoning to him. He gathered them into his large hands in order to roll them around and around. Shinar noticed what he was doing; she stared at his hands. Raf became self-conscious. He immediately took his hands out of his pockets to show the nuclear diamonds to Shinar. She looked down to see his open hands holding the stones.

She gasped. "Are those…?"

He talked over her. "Yeah, they're Azazel stones," he said in a matter-of-fact way.

Shinar couldn't take her eyes off them. "I've never seen them outside the display at the Anackim temple."

Shinar looked as if she would like to hold one herself. To Raf, her interest was palpable. He dumped all the stones from one of his hands to the other, save one that he gave to Shinar. She became fascinated! Thoughts of eating left her mind. She touched it with her free hand, caressing it with her fingertips.

"Order for Shi," came a voice from the other side of the counter. She snapped to. Her focus turned toward their food, though she didn't let go of the stone. Shinar wrapped her fingers around it as she grabbed the food tray with her other hand. She tried to appear nonchalant while carrying their meal to a table. She'd instantly felt drawn to the nuclear diamond. It represented many dimensions of important aspects to her life. The past came alive in her hand. This artifact also added some credibility to Raf's existence as well as his story about Super Earth. It also provided a tangible feeling through her skin; the energy of the uranium-like substance inside exuded warmth. The nuclear diamond became friendly to her.

Raf recognized Shi's attraction to the stone. "You can keep that one if you like."

She was almost startled. "Oh, this, a… Okay, sure, thanks." She tried to appear casual but couldn't hide her desire for it. "Thanks, Raf.

It's really cool."

His nervousness was starting to subside a bit. "It doesn't make us engaged or anything."

Raf hadn't tried humor for a long time. He was hoping Shinar would appreciate his effort. She seemed to. He could almost swear she blushed a little while displaying a hint of a smile.

Shinar finally deposited the nuclear diamond in her own pocket so she could eat lunch.

*****

After initially being startled, Resnik became very pleased. It was time to apply the password he'd been given. Seven digits later brought him access to the Epygen files. He quickly began digging for pertinent information about Kaylee. Resnik bypassed files about himself, at least for now. Time was tight; he needed to keep moving. A major file simply entitled "Isha" came into view. He clicked on it. A picture led his journey into the file. It was a much cleaner and slightly fatter version of the girl once named Isha. Pictures of an egg and sperm came next, followed by technical information. Resnik took cell phone pics from the monitor screen. Yasti remained on the lookout for any intruders. A deeper search showed images of a surgical table with a young girl on it lying face down. Sek was shown in the background watching the procedure. He looked older, not younger, in those images. Others in the scenes were wearing lab coats. Resnik was looking for information that might push A. L. Sek into losing interest in Kaylee.

"I can hear people," said Yasti. She rushed to the door to have a peek.

Resnik quickly snapped a few pics of what he deemed useful objectives. He was about to end his search.

Yasti urgently indicated for Resnik to shut it down immediately.

He now did as directed, then scrambled to find a place to hide. The two of them noticed a bathroom close by; in they went. They could hear the door open. Both were hoping to be left alone in their hiding place.

"They've got her," said someone with a very pleasing and very persuasive male voice. "Looks like you've actually managed to fulfill your obligation, Sek."

Sek remained silent. Over time, he'd realized trying to explain, to make excuses, just got him in trouble. Even when things looked good for him, he kept his mouth shut.

Resnik could hear the computer firing up once again. Yasti was cupping her ear with her hand so as to listen carefully to what was going on just outside their hiding spot.

"No, bring her here! I want to see the morphing myself," said the unknown and unseen voice.

Resnik derived a sinking feeling while eavesdropping on Sek and his companion. *Could they be talking about my daughter?*

Emotions turned to adrenaline. He wanted to expose himself immediately to find out if they were talking about Kaylee. Logic held him back. What good would it do? He was powerless against Sek and his people. Even with Yasti and her weapons, the evil and might of Epygen could easily conceal Kaylee. A different strategy would have to be enacted. An outrageous thought came into his head. Resnik turned his head to glance at Yasti. He then raised his hand, palm facing her, as to beckon Yasti to stay. She understood. She also recognized the look in his eyes; they silently said, "Stay and fight another day." He stood up from his crouching position and walked out of the bathroom. Stepping onto an undiscovered planet, moon, or star was easier than what he was about to embark upon. Willfully surrendering himself to a Guardian while having the blessings of the Messenger was something he could deal with. Giving himself up to an ego-driven man was altogether different. Once again, Resnik took a moment to connect with the Spirit before entering onto this dangerous path. After a few moments, the Spirit within gave him the boldness and protection he needed.

Resnik now had the confidence to move forward.

He walked out of the bathroom from which he was hiding and offered himself to A. L. Sek. Resnik was immediately apprehended by Sek's people. The act of coming forth held an unexpected benefit. The mysterious voice talking down to Sek now possessed a face. He was much taller than AL. The handsome man had white skin and streaks of gray mingled in black hair. His thick beard was trimmed very precisely so as to look slightly devilish. The deep color of his eyes seemed to absorb light. Faint tones of reddish-auburn were present in the irises. Something else emanated from this charismatic man; a powerful aura of pride seemed to encapsulate his demeanor. Being in his presence for only a few seconds enticed Resnik to be subservient to this stranger. Resnik was able to counter these emotional subtleties with the help of the Spirit.

The stranger spoke. "Who are you, sir?"

A. L. Sek started to chime in. "He's—"

The stranger cut off Sek. "I'm glad you've decided to join us. I'm known as the Prophet."

Resnik was pretty sure the Prophet knew who he is. He obliged the Prophet nonetheless.

"I'm Resnik Clayborn."

Prophet continued his sly questioning. "It's interesting that we meet in this unique place."

Resnik was silently stoic.

Prophet raised his head slightly while quietly talking. "Two family members," he subtly uttered to himself, with the others listening.

Prophet now spoke boldly while turning to walk away. "Bring him!"

Resnik was taken!

*****

Gettie got back to the farmhouse as quickly as possible. He was distraught! His mind was racing. Who took his wife? How did he get her back? He could almost guess the answer to the first question. *Epygen,* he thought. California became his number one destination. He got on his cell phone to order an airplane. Next, he tried calling his father—no answer. His mom was also unavailable. Gettie decided to make his way straight to Epygen's corporate headquarters by any means possible.

*****

Neko signed papers. She wasn't quite sure how to collect her new belongings. She thought, *There will be enough time later to dwell on newfound acquisitions.*

For now, she turned her attention to the cell phone in her purse. Gettie's urgent text and call came into focus. Panic tried to overwhelm her! She was quickly reminded that the Spirit had been her ally for the past many years. Neko focused on that fact to ease her emotions. Her cell phone indicated Gettie was on a plane. Kaylee was missing! Talking to her husband was now paramount, and she realized he might be incommunicado while undercover.

She thought hard. *I do have my own aircraft.*

That decision was easy. Within the hour, she was on her way to California. The slumbering warrior in her was awakened. Neko hadn't realized that side of herself for a long time. Memories of her childhood came to her mind's eye. Kicking ass in martial arts class while fighting boys much bigger than herself began getting her pumped. Saving Resnik's life was also an adrenaline-worthy memory. Perhaps the best fight seen in her mind was beating up William Parti while on *Derecho*. She could still hear the sounds of slaps and thuds emanating from his body as she laid into him. Confidence was building in her heart. The family she loved so much was depending on her.

Time to put on my big girl panties! Neko bent her will into saving her loved ones.

The Den of Iniquity

Raf and Shinar made their way to the Anackim temple. He was once again stirred from deep within to interact with his newfound family. The walk to the temple was crowned with delight as Shinar held Raf's hand. He bonded with her in a way he'd never contemplated before. She seemed to fill any gaps in his personality. Shinar was confident socially; Raf was withdrawn and somewhat awkward in one-on-one interactions. He never wanted to be without Shinar, whether on Earth or Purgatory. *Maybe Earth could be my new home. After all, my newfound family dwell here*, he thought. Unbeknownst to his conscious thoughts, his mind was now fully prepared for what would come next. The Fallen were having a powerful influence on Raf. Pride had also attempted to affect Raf through the atmospheric barrier on Purgatory.

Raf and Shinar rounded the last corner and came to a blank wall that had no visible door. Raf raised the GPS card, turning it upside down. "Watchers" was lit up on the card and simultaneously displayed on the wall. They entered, anticipating another warm welcome. They were not disappointed; Reen was waiting to greet them. Another man was with him. This other man was as friendly as a politician, with looks to match. Shinar had met him before, though she deferred the introduction to Reen.

"Raf, this is my good friend the Prophet. Prophet, this is my kin, Raf," indicated Reen.

Raf put his hand out to offer a friendly embrace. The Prophet reciprocated. "I'm known as the Prophet, but please, my friends just call me Prophet."

Raf responded as he'd been taught. "Nice to meet you, Prophet."

Prophet continued. "I'm very glad to meet you, young man." Prophet shook Raf's hand vigorously. "Can I show you something? I have a special opportunity just for you."

Shinar ever so slightly squeezed Raf's hand in an act of encouragement. Raf agreed to indulge Prophet in his offer. The four of them proceeded to an isolated room in the building.

Raf became astonished! An enormous map of the world was displayed on a massive digital screen. The room is centered around the screen in a half-circle configuration. Very large tables were assembled as workstations, all oriented to view the screen. The setting is impressive. This first viewing for Raf left him in awe and filled him with questions.

Prophet was reading Raf's facial expressions. "This is all for you, son. We would like your help."

Raf was speechless. He thought, *Who am I to utilize this tech? I went to school for political science and business management, not IT*. He just stared at the impressive equipment.

Prophet chimed in again. "Don't let all this overwhelm you. We have people who run this room. I need you for something a little different." He could tell Raf was at a loss for words. "Your brethren and I would like you to consider helping us help the world."

Raf was now even more dumbfounded! Though he assumed when Prophet mentioned *brethren*, he was talking about descendants of the Nephilim like himself. *But what does Prophet need, and who is he, really?* he thought.

Raf gave Shinar a glance. Her face was unwavering, her hand still in his. He ventured a little more down the rabbit hole.

"What can I do for you?" asked Raf while looking at Prophet with scrutinizing eyes.

"Everything!"

*****

Neko landed. She had no interest in noticing the extravagant luxury of her newly acquired aircraft. Her focus was intent upon a mission to uncover evil. *Where to start?* she thought. Epygen was the obvious choice. *Do I just walk through the front door? They know who I am. They will know why I'm here.* She paused to think it over.

Neko tried texting her son once more. "r u in CA?" She was relieved to get a quick reply.

"I'm almost to Epygen's headquarters," was his return text.

She wasn't completely surprised to hear he had zeroed in on Epygen. Neko began developing a plan. She knew Qusay wanted— even needed—her knowledge of energy. She also realized he had an association with A. L. Sek. "I'll leverage my abilities against the safety and return of Kaylee," she thought.

Gettie was now very close to the entry of Epygen. Neko had also just arrived in an Uber. Both were ecstatic to see each other. They embraced.

"They've got her, Mom! She's probably right inside that building." He was ready to barnstorm Epygen.

"I know, sweetheart. I think I have a way for them to invite us in."

She raised her cell phone to send a text. "I've got what you want." Neko sent the message to Qusay.

Qusay had an adrenaline spike! His thoughts were in hyperdrive. He'd been working on a way to extract information from Neko. Was she now willing to give it freely? *Or perhaps she's going to denounce her unjustified inheritance!* he thought.

His narcissistic heart was bent on greed. He paused his excitement for a moment. *Does she already know about the abduction of the red- headed girl?* He wasn't sure of the exact reason Neko was reaching out to him, so he planned on playing it cool.

Qusay replied without delay. "Mrs. Clayborn, how can I assist you?"

"You want to obtain the secrets of energy. I know what it is!" She actually didn't fully know—at least, not yet.

However, she was close—very, very close. Neko was counting on Qusay's unrelenting selfishness to pull him into her trap.

Qusay wasn't waiting for her to say another word. He could tell she was outside Epygen's main office complex by an alert on his phone. He invited her to enter the building. Two security guards were immediately dispatched. They exited the front doors with fervor in order to escort Neko and Gettie inside. So far Neko's plan was off to a great start. Although there was more at stake than just dealing with Qusay. He was only the first part of her scheme. She would need to remain sanguine throughout the entire process. Being calm and collected would also be necessary. Neko chose to rely on the Spirit for the fortitude to deal with all of it.

"Stay close, son. I've got a plan. They know we know about Kaylee. Stay humble, emotions under control," were her last words to Gettie before entering "the den of iniquity" (Epygen).

*****

Yasti emailed Palmer, requesting more weapons. "Wilson can't land on Earth. They're after *Ornan*," was his return email.

Shock went through her! What was she to do without an escape plan? Yasti dug a little deeper into her emotions. "Stay calm," she said to herself. Yasti wanted to help. She just wasn't sure how to do it. She decided to beckon the Spirit. "I need you! Please help me!" was her cry. This wasn't her first time turning to the Spirit in a time of need. She just didn't always choose to ask for assistance. She often tried to tough it out and shoulder the burden on her own. Though it always went better with help from the Spirit. He was like a friend, a best friend, that would make a real difference.

This time she had waited until the circumstance was desperate. Really, she knew better than to postpone such a request, she too often tried to go it alone. Not this time! Her task was extremely urgent.

After only a few moments of communicating with the Spirit, Yasti acquired clarity. Patience was called for. She simply hunkered down in Sek's office, in the bathroom, waiting for the right opportunity to act. Peace consoled her for now. The Spirit seemed to be telling her, "As difficult as it may seem, sometimes waiting is the best course of action."

*****

Everything. Raf contemplated that word for a moment. *Does Prophet think I possess some sort of power?* he thought. Raf decided to ask Prophet for a further explanation. "What do you mean, sir?"

"I want you to lead us into the future." Prophet's countenance was very sincere.

At this point, Shinar added her other hand to Raf's arm as a further show of support.

Raf beckoned again to Prophet. "Lead the Anackim?" he asked.

Prophet was very stoic. "Yes. And everyone else. We're designing *a new world order*. We think you're the perfect man for the job."

Raf was speechless. He thought Prophet's proposal was ridiculous. Yet Prophet had an aura about him. It was like he could persuade *anyone* to do his bidding. Raf's mind was being pulled into the desires of Prophet.

He considered Prophet's outrageous request.

"*A new world order*, what does that *look* like?" asked Raf.

Prophet gladly responded. "Not unlike your Purgatory. The poor are supported by the wealthy, and the government provides for the people. And we oversee everyone."

Raf was abashed. He knew Purgatory wasn't the way Prophet described it. The City in Space was established as a community of love for one another, not a subservient society. As for the rest of what Prophet was preaching, Raf mulled it over in his mind. He knew Earth was struggling. *But did it need such an extreme solution? And would Prophet's solution really work?* His initial thoughts told him Prophet is full of it. However, something intangible was gnawing at Raf's emotions. Once again, Prophet's powerful aura was chipping away at Raf's resolve. He reached into his pocket with his free hand to connect with the nuclear diamonds. They were his comfort, he now *counted* on them to soothe him. The room went silent. Prophet's skills kicked in. He gave Raf space to think. Prophet engaged his subtle gift in order to persuade Raf during the silence. The nuclear diamonds were also working on Raf's emotions. They beckoned him into a state of euphoria. These two invisible forces combined to invoke a powerful lure in Raf's mind. His infatuation with Shinar was also adding a degree of capitulation to his decision-making process. She was unwavering in her desire for Raf to attain this new level of leadership. He desired *that* kind of power himself. In his heart, he always wanted it. *But was this the right way to get it?* he thought.

The nuclear diamonds felt good in his hand. Shinar's hands felt good on his arm. The persuasion that came from the patience of Prophet would also not be denied. Raf decided to venture further toward this new opportunity. He agreed to see more of what Prophet had to offer. Raf nodded his head in agreement.

Since he had no free hand to shake, Prophet squeezed Raf's large shoulder as a sign of compliance.

"Come with me, *son*." Raf was comforted by that designation to himself. Resnik would also use the word *son* to young men other than Gettie as a term of affection.

Prophet led Raf and Shinar to another room. The room was much smaller than the enormous *media* room they had just exited. It looked like a medical examination room. Reen stayed outside. Raf once again looked to Shinar, who seemed to be okay with all that was happening.

Prophet immediately offered up another request; he wasn't waiting for Raf to vacillate. "I have a small favor to ask of you. We would like you to always be connected to your family. There is a microchip that will allow communication between you and the monitoring room we were just in. Through Ansible, you will have the ability to talk to Shinar or Reen or anyone else you choose, from anywhere, at any time, even while you're on Purgatory."

Raf had a few questions of his own. "Is there some sort of microphone on it?"

Prophet answered in a manner that was slightly elevated from his usual calm demeanor. "No, but that's the beauty of it. You just think to it. The chip is very advanced!"

Knock...knock...knock. Someone on the other side of the door was asking to enter.

"Please come in," uttered Prophet.

The door opened; it wasn't Reen, he was gone. Another man accompanied by a woman entered, both wearing doctor's smocks. They brought a small container along with a few sterilized surgical instruments. The items were placed close to where Raf was standing. The container was opened, revealing what looked like a small grain of sand. Upon closer examination, an incredibly small cube-shaped microchip could be seen.

Prophet now gave an explanation. "This is a graphene computer chip with nanowire transistors. It's the newest technology. It will ensure your ability to talk with Shinar from any location you happen to find yourself in."

Prophet had relish in his voice. He studied Raf's face to ascertain any uncertainty. Raf just stared at the chip. Prophet continued. "It goes under your skin."

Raf contemplated all that was happening. Putting this tiny *thing* under his skin seemed a small price to pay in order to stay in communication to the beautiful woman holding his arm. He didn't ever want to go without being connected to Shinar. Being on Purgatory and out of reach with his new love was an unpleasant memory he never wanted to repeat.

Prophet again waited patiently while Raf thought.

After a few additional moments, Raf's eyes connected to Prophet's. He then raised the arm Shinar wasn't holding to offer it for chip insertion.

"No, son, it goes under your hairline, on the back of your head," stated Prophet.

Raf instinctively touched his head, wondering exactly where it would go.

Sensing Raf's cooperation, Prophet seized every opportunity to keep his scheme in play. "Please have a seat. It will just take a moment."

Raf was still entranced by the woman at his side and the power of Prophet. Also, thoughts of leadership *at a high level* were pulling him into this dynamic. He submitted to Prophet's wishes once again. In only a few minutes, the chip was implanted behind Raf's right ear, under his skin. Once the procedure was finished, Raf looked up at Shinar. She had an "I'm proud of you" look on her face. She even lightly touched the back of his head with her hand while displaying a gentle smile.

Prophet smoothly gave more direction. "Let's go back to the media room. We'll activate the chip there."

The completion of Prophet's goal was just seconds away. Raf had no *real* idea of the magnitude of what was about to happen. Shinar, Raf, and Prophet joined Reen, who was sitting in front of a keypad inside the media and monitoring room.

"Please have a seat," offered Reen.

Raf sat alongside Reen in a very comfortable oversized chair that seemed to be just his size. Reen motioned Raf to look up at the enormous screen displaying telemetry of data received from the chip in Raf's skull. So far, all readouts were at zero.

Reen spoke again. "I'm going to activate the chip now; you may feel a small twinge."

Raf mentally braced himself. He did feel something! A minor shock emanated from just behind his right ear. His right eye twitched a bit. He prepared for pain, but none came. Instead, pleasure was felt. Unbeknownst to Raf, a time-released hit of dopamine entered his brain while simultaneously the chip *fired up*! Raf liked it! He now associated the *activated* chip with pleasure. Epygen's experiment was working. Telemetry started being displayed on the media screen. All of Raf's vital signs could also be seen. His location also appeared. Much more data began showing up, though it was all encrypted. He did, however, notice some relatively small words on the bottom right corner of the huge screen: "Made by Epygen, ID #0.666." Raf glanced at Reen for an explanation.

"It's just compiling information. It will take time for it to display everything in a language we can understand." No mention of the manufacturer was given.

Reen was not being 100 percent honest with Raf. He knew the chip was connecting to the Internet as well as deeply connecting to Raf's mind. The chip is capable of doing even more than Reen was aware of. He changed the subject. "Say something," he indicated to Raf.

"Hello." His voice came booming through the sound system. Shinar looked around with a surprised look on her face.

Reen now asked Raf to *think it*, instead of verbally speaking it.

Raf cooperated by keeping his mouth silent. "Hello!" Raf's synthesized voice came through the speakers once again. This time, the quality of his voice was slightly *computer*-like. It still sounded like him, just subtly *machine*-ish.

Shinar and Raf looked at each other in astonishment! Without pausing to think it through, he mentally spoke again, *I love you, Shinar!*

"I love you, Shinar!" was displayed on the gigantic screen along with a synthesized version of Raf's deep, commanding voice.

All four were surprised at the compulsiveness of Raf. Shinar's face turned a shade darker. She covered her mouth with her hand. She then whispered in his ear, "I love you too."

Raf's microchip experience was off to a surprisingly delightful start! He even felt a little empowered, though he had no idea how much power had been given to him, or what that power would entail.

*****

Resnik was taken to a well-guarded room deep within Epygen. He wasn't treated badly, yet.

"Don't let him touch you," ordered A. L. Sek. He knew Resnik could *heal* with his hands, although... *Could he also harm?* wondered Sek. He didn't want to find out.

The guards were afraid to touch Resnik anywhere, so he sat by himself. The guards surrounding him had weapons loaded and pointed at his vitals. Resnik was very concerned about himself and his daughter, yet he focused on the Spirit for peace and comfort while in this confined state. Discouragement and fear were confronting him as well. He stayed mentally focused on the Spirit to get him through.

"We should eliminate him," said Sek.

Qusay once again fired back at Sek with a belittling statement. "No, I thought you were supposed to be smart."

The prince couldn't believe his luck! This was his backup plan all along. He thought he might need to kidnap Resnik in order to force Neko into continuing her energy research. He was feeling pretty *cocky* at this point.

"Just hold him, if you can manage that without fucking up!" stated Qusay, condescendingly.

Sek cowered once again. He barely managed to keep himself from sassing back at Qusay.

*****

Kaylee was back where she started, and she was scared! Her goal to *work through* her fears backfired. Now an even bigger fear transpired! She felt foolish…and horrified at the thought of coming face-to-face with Sek. Kaylee's so-called *father*, turned out to be more evil than she would have imagined. Meeting him again was now imminent. She tried to mentally prepare herself, but her emotions kept getting in the way. Kaylee was near to having a panic attack.

A familiar but dreaded voice sounded behind her. "So this is what you've become."

Unfortunately, Kaylee knew the man who belonged to it. A. L. Sek came into the science lab, where she was bound. With a jolt of adrenaline, she remembered what her husband had shared with her. The Spirit was a very present help in time of need.

If there was ever a need for help, it is now, Kaylee thought.

Before she could say a word to Sek, she connected to the Spirit. Amazingly, peace entered her torn emotions. Kaylee was all alone against Sek, yet she now felt supported. A little confidence was also building. She even went a step further… and offered *grace* to her captor.

Kaylee went from nervous and shaking to having a semblance of calm. "Thank you for giving me life." She said this with a hint of boldness in her voice.

Sek was taken aback. Such moxie was not expected from the skinny girl he'd once known. He was speechless for a moment but recovered quickly. "You were an experiment. You're still an experiment. We're going to study you further."

"I'm damaged now. My dominant DNA is no longer prevalent. We've interrupted your master plan," answered Kaylee with resolve in her voice.

Sek was desperately trying to come to terms with what Kaylee pointed out. He knew she was correct. After all, she looked different from the way Epygen had designed her. And who's the "we" she was talking about? He paused for a moment. The answer came to his mind. *There is only one conclusion: Resnik Clayborn!* Sek felt there was also only *one* solution.

"I can fix that," he said to Kaylee with his usual smug attitude.

Sek left Kaylee alone so he could enact a new directive.

*****

Yasti was so calmed by the Spirit that she had fallen asleep hiding in A. L. Sek's private bathroom. She awoke with fervor and a clear picture of what she needed to do. Resnik is her primary concern; however, will she be able to find him? Then, how do they get back to Purgatory? Yasti had to forgo rescuing him in order to first secure *Ornan*'s landing dock.

158

How to get out of Epygen without being detected? she thought.

She grabbed a bunch of towels from the bathroom. Her ruse was to pretend to be housekeeping. The oversized clothes she was wearing could easily be mistaken for cleaning garb. Yasti set off on her mission. Exploring the building on her way out became part of her plan. She would glance in on every door that was open. She also tried to memorize the floor plan as best as she could. Yasti even found where they keep cleaning carts. She gained in confidence while pushing a cart down Epygen's hallways.

A stray thought entered her mind: *What if I dig a little deeper?*

She began exploring additional floors in the building. A service elevator indicated subfloors. The cleaning cart had a designated cubby that contained keys. One of the keys looked unique, like a small round tube with a notch at the end. Yasti tried it in the elevator wall. She simply turned the key in the direction of the indicated floor. The elevator went downward. She went deep into the den of Epygen. Yasti discerned if the cart had subfloor keys, then housekeeping also went there. She now fell back to her original task and began hunting for her friend, Resnik. She went to the lowest floor first. A wealth of weapons beneath her garments could not dispel a certain fear building in her heart. Something in the depths of Epygen felt so different from her life on Purgatory. She was sensing evil. Yasti knew evil; she'd seen it up close and personal on the Dark Planet, TrES-2b. The feeling of being in the presence of evil was palpable, even though she hadn't laid eyes on anything yet. Yasti ventured further into the hallway directly in front of the opening elevator doors. A distinct smell emanated from this basement, not of concrete but of living creatures and chemicals. She was cautious, listening intently.

Animals way down here? Yasti thought.

The smell in this subterranean place mimicked animals she'd grown up around. Yasti knew the smell of monkeys and cows, even the odor of tiger droppings. Some of the cities in India were close to the jungle. Curiosity was driving her forward more than the fear of what she may encounter, though she kept one hand on a cocked weapon inside her loose-fitting clothes. A door suddenly opened! This gave her a small pulse of adrenaline. A person wearing a lab coat scurried into the hall several feet from Yasti. She tried not to overreact. She looked down at the cleaning cart, attempting to look preoccupied. As the lab tech passed by, Yasti risked a glance upward. It was like she was invisible. The man in the lab coat just passed by in a nonchalant manner. This gave her a bit more confidence in her ruse. She waited until the man was out of sight, then looked inside the freshly shut door. The animal smell increased exponentially! And now odd sounds could be heard. She stepped inside the room, propping open the door with the cart.

It looks more official this way, she thought. *Besides, it might slow down someone reentering the room.*

Cages now came into view. Some were like dog kennel crates, others much bigger. Every one of them had an animal inside. Yasti was taken aback. These animals were unfamiliar to any creature she'd seen, whether at a zoo or nature show. She risked a quick glance at several cages; time wasn't a luxury she could indulge in. One animal that stood out from the rest, possessed both feathers and fur. Yasti mulled over the image in her mind: "Is that an enormous owl or a large cat?" The creature had a large head that mimicked an owl, but with a flat face and mouth like a Persian house cat. This animal was the size of a lion. Its head is brilliantly wreathed in a plethora of feathers that faded into fur as they progressed toward the tail. Yasti wanted to touch it.

She approached. "Are you friendly?" she held out her hand. The animal's incredibly large eyes connected to hers. The eyes didn't turn in their sockets; the owl-cat had to turn its head to look in different directions.

It appeared to be nonaggressive. Yasti got closer. Without warning, the creature screeched! It was an ear-shattering sound! The noise started as a high-pitched bird-of-prey cry that resonated with a tone of a lion's roar. That was enough for Yasti. She took that as her cue to move on. She paused for a quick look around. Fortunately, no one else could be seen. The cleaning cart was moved into the hallway as she exited the room of cages.

If that was in the first door, what's at the end of the hall? thought Yasti.

Time was beckoning to her, but she wanted one last look. She moved quickly to the final door. This one was locked. Yasti grabbed the cluster of keys and began searching for those that looked important. After a few tries with several larger keys, the lock turned. Once again, she held open the entry door with the cart. Only a brief peek was warranted. However, it only took a glance for Yasti to want so much more. The room opened up to a wide viewing window that overlooked a vast subterranean desert. Saguaro cactuses were sprinkled about, along with the occasional mesquite tree. Large boulders were also strewn here and there. She also noticed a few small patches of green. Grass was growing under the artificial lights. Nevertheless, the foliage was only a side note to what really caught her eye. More animals were moving around, freely this time. Yasti became appalled! These creatures were even more shocking in appearance than the caged animals.

They're some mutated form of life, she thought.

They could only be described as human deviation. Some seemed to have the face of a man and the body of a dog. Others displayed the body of a person with the head of a monkey.

The deformed beings were randomly moving about, unclothed in the warm environment. Judging from their movements, they didn't seem to have the intelligence quotient of a normal human. Yasti was fascinated by the sight of this phenomenon, yet it sickened her.

She pulled herself away from the large overlook. Time was up! She really needed to keep moving. The cart was moved out of the doorway as Yasti reentered the hallway. After taking only a few steps, an angry voice was heard.

"Ah-ha, I caught you!"

*****

Neko was welcomed "graciously" by Prince Qusay. She felt it was like the old days when he wanted to possess her, although she suspected he would change his tune quickly.

"Can I get you anything?" offered Qusay.

Gettie had a look of loathing on his face. Qusay avoided eye contact with Neko's son. As far as Qusay was concerned, Gettie was every bit Resnik's son. And the prince wasn't about to test Gettie's powers, if any existed. Staying an arm's length away from his rival's son was Qusay's protocol.

Neko accepted Qusay's offer. "I'll take some coffee." She was buying some time to fulfill her plan. Gettie kept his mouth shut; he was unsure of how best to play along with his mother's plan. He took a path of being congenial even though he wanted to beat Qusay to death. Gettie also felt the Spirit calming him. He realized waiting for the opportune moment would be *key* to rescuing his beloved Kaylee. Gettie went a step further and put all his trust in the Spirit, even to the smallest detail of his current situation.

Coffee was brought out for all three individuals. It seemed Qusay was attempting to be "chummy" with his enemies. Neko attempted to display a demeanor of confidence. Like her son, she wanted to throttle Qusay by applying her martial arts skills to his hide.

She comforted herself by thinking, *I may still kick his ass later*.

Neko held Qusay in the palm of her hand, at least for now. She had what he wanted. Now it was time to turn the tables on him. She asked for an electronic tablet in order to map out an equation. Qusay was enticed; he gladly obliged Neko. She began formulating important- looking equations on the notepad. These calculations weren't all that Qusay was hoping for. He also wanted Neko to redact the inheritance from his father. He watched intently while she typed. The statements looked good and seemed legitimate, but Neko held back key pieces from the prince. This wasn't too difficult; she didn't quite have everything needed to complete her formulation of what energy is. Like others, she knew what energy could do, but what exactly was it? And how could she label it, then even exploit it further? She was close to answering these questions. If she was successful in solving this awesome problem, would that be worth the lives of her loved ones?

After twenty years of working for Sheik Kahlil, Neko got to know his son, or at least knew Qusay's character. She knew his eyes were on the tablet. She enticed him further. She added details concerning the inheritance. As Neko typed, it appeared she was about to renounce her recently acquired assets. She could hear Qusay's breath becoming elevated.

Suddenly Neko stopped pressing the keys. Her eyes moved from the electric notepad to Qusay.

Her face was stern. "Bring me Resnik and Kaylee!"

*****

Raf now wondered what to do next. *Should I tell my Purgatory family about the chip?* he thought. After pondering it for a few moments, he decided to withhold his new experience from them, at least for now.

His urge to share his new acquisition would have to stay with Shinar for the time being. Besides, in his mind, she was now his family. He took one more glance at the giant media screen; most of what appeared was still encrypted. Raf got up from his chair to leave the media room with Shinar in tow. He paused in the doorway to ask one final question. "How do I turn it off?"

Reen answered, "Just say or think the word *Mammon*. You should hear an audible tone, indicating that it's been put into a wait state. To turn it back on, say or think *Mammon wake*."

Raf was excited at being able to connect with Shinar or the Nephilim anytime he wanted. So much so that he trusted Reen without question. He was hungry and ready for a substantial meal. He said his good-byes to Reen and Prophet. Shinar also said farewell to Reen and Prophet, thanking them as well. She was a substantial-sized woman herself and gladly obliged Raf in finding a nearby restaurant. As they walked the streets of Dubai, Raf reached up to the back of his head to feel the newly implanted chip. He embraced the idea of it almost as much as the nuclear diamonds in his pocket. He couldn't remember a time when he felt more comforted. Everything and everyone other than the chip, the diamonds, and Shinar seemed distant. His feelings toward his mom and his surrogate brother were also fading. Even Resnik and the City in Space were a million miles away in Raf's emotions.

Old-fashioned steak and potatoes were on the menu for the young couple. A private corner booth was found in a very nice Wagyu steak house. Raf was pleasantly surprised once again when Shinar sat next to him. He wasn't used to so much feminine attention. The fact that she's from his Nephilim family pleased him even more. For the first time in his life, Raf began contemplating a physical relationship with the opposite sex. He allowed himself to drop his guard around Shinar. He embraced the idea of looking at her with desire in his heart. The only thing stopping him from kissing her was lack of experience. Raf decided he could at least muster up enough courage to put his arm around Shinar. He lifted his left arm in a slightly awkward, unnatural manner as to rest it on her shoulder. She acknowledged this by scooting in closer to him. He loved feeling Shinar's body close to his and she smelled good. Raf's confidence was building. He began envisioning Shinar joining himself in his hotel room after dinner. Two glasses of water interrupted Raf's train of thought.

"Good evening, my name is Steve. Can I get you something to drink other than water?"

Steve had the look of awe written all over his face. Raf tried to ignore it. This wasn't the first person on earth to assume he was a basketball player. Raf anticipated a request for an autograph before the meal is over. On Purgatory he was humble and a bit awkward. On Earth he was thrust into a world of ego-stroking. While there, Raf was being bombarded by pride at a high level. He embraced the feeling. After all, why not? Maybe he deserved to have things go his way. *How could something that feels this good be bad?* he thought.

Food was placed before him and Shinar. Raf had to decide whether or not to eat with only his right arm. He opted to remove his left arm from around Shinar in order to eat properly.

*****

Resnik was biding his time. He had confidence in the Spirit. In his heart, he felt it was just a matter of time until he knew exactly what to do. And there was no doubt in his mind that Yasti was working on some sort of plan to help him. Resnik remained calm but ready to act at a moment's notice.

*****

Kaylee's inner peace continued to build. Positive thoughts began entering her mind. She was reminded of the journey that brought her back to this place. When she first escaped Epygen, fear motivated her actions. Then confidence slowly came to the surface of her emotions. She ventured out in search of Resnik Clayborn by herself. She traveled a great distance unaided. Isha fended for herself over a substantial period. She mustered enough courage to allow Resnik to modify her DNA. Perhaps her return trip to Earth really has brought healing to her soul. If she could make it through all that, maybe she could handle whatever A. L. Sek could dish out.

*****

Yasti froze! Had she been found out? She cautiously inserted her hand in the loose-fitting clothes she was wearing. Her hand landed on one of the weapons she had concealed.

"I'm talking to you!" The voice behind her had become even more elevated. Yasti slowly started to turn around. Adrenaline was flowing through her veins! The safety on the hidden weapon was now clicked to the off position.

"I told you guys not to clean down here at this time of the day!"

Another click was heard as the safety on the weapon was moved back into the on position. Yasti was very relieved. She responded to the angry voice in a subservient manner.

"I'm sorry, sir, it won't happen again. Once I made it to the end of the hallway, I realized the time and turned back."

The aggressive man who belonged to the belittling voice seemed to be satisfied with Yasti's statement. He concluded with, "Yeah, if you do it again, I'll tell your boss!" She went on her way, anxious to not be noticed again. Any new doors she encountered were delicately and quietly cracked open so as to just glimpse inside. She wouldn't risk entering a strange room anymore as she continued to stay focused on her quest to find Resnik.

*****

As anticipated, the waiter left a request along with the check for their meal. It was on an additional piece of paper: "Can I have your autograph? It's for a friend of mine. His name is Steve."

Raf knew the waiter's name to be Steve; he indulged him nonetheless. Raf signed, "Rafykei Wombosie, to my friend Steve." A quick glance as Raf and Shinar left the restaurant showed Steve ogling over the fresh autograph. With full stomachs, the couple made their way to the ocean so they could relax by the shoreline. The sound of water rolling onto the sand was settling to their souls. This exciting day had increased the bond between each other. Shinar took her shoes off so as to feel the sand on her bare feet. Raf thought about doing the same. When she rolled up her pants so they wouldn't get wet, he thought about other things. He was geared up from the extraordinary day and his ego was pumped up. Confidence was boosting his desire to see more of Shinar.

She noticed him staring at her legs. "Do you want to sit down on those rocks?" she indicated an outcropping close to where they were standing. The large boulders were easy to manage. Shinar waited for Raf to recline before joining him. She was sensitive to his inexperience. Shinar approached Raf gracefully, putting her right leg between both of his. She then sat down landing her left leg next to his right arm. He once again focused his eyes on the uncovered portion of her body. Shinar took Raf's hand into her own and placed it on her left leg.

"This is just for you," she said in a soft, soothing voice.

Raf responded to Shinar's initiative and began exploring her calf by squeezing and rubbing it. She moved her right foot a little closer to his groin. He put his free hand on that leg to caress it as well. Shinar tilted her head back and closed her eyes to indicate the pleasure and physical closeness she was feeling. Raf was also caught up in the moment. It didn't take long for him to realize he wanted more. Shinar leaned in toward Raf to offer a kiss. He gladly obliged. Their passion was ignited that evening under the moonlight with the ocean waves crashing against the rock they were sitting on.

*****

Qusay contemplated Neko's request. He desperately wanted the information she held. He paused for a few moments, then turned toward one of his bodyguards and whispered a command: "Bring Clayborn and the girl."

Immediately the man left to retrieve the two hostages. Neko's eyes followed them out of the room. She wasn't about to hand over critical information prematurely. She stood her ground and waited patiently. Neko also realized the Spirit would be her ally if and when her loved ones were brought into her presence. A possible dangerous situation could easily arise; in fact, she was planning on it.

The bodyguard entered the lab where Kaylee was being restrained. She snapped to. She had become so relaxed that a nap had overwhelmed her. She became startled but not scared as the large man disabled the restraints that were holding her to the chair. His large hand encompassed the entirety of her wrist as he once again restrained her. Kaylee was fast but not strong. She had no choice other than to go with him. Kaylee comforted herself by indulging in thoughts of being reunited with her family, though in reality, she had no idea where this guard was taking her.

The crackling on-and-off sounds of a two-way radio were heard along with muddled voices. The men surrounding Resnik were on the move. They became more intense with their weapons, motioning Resnik to move to a different location. He cooperated willingly. He felt others in his landing party may also be in harm's way. He wasn't about to do anything risky. He remained cool-headed and calm.

The commotion of their movements caught the attention of Yasti who was still wandering the hallways. She quickly gained mobility to catch up to the man she was sent to protect. As she increased her pace, adrenaline once again filled her veins. Yasti relished finding Resnik. In her heart, she knew the Spirit was helping her. She quickly attempted to count the number of men escorting Resnik. The six men all had significant weapons and stayed beyond an arm's reach of her friend. They seemed to give her no mind, though Yasti's pace allowed her to close in on them.

She gave thought to reaching within her loose-fitting clothes and pulling out a few weapons of her own. Incomplete knowledge of an escape plan caused her to hesitate. Yasti followed the seven men just short of the door they entered. She once again employed extreme caution as the door shut. Charging into the unknown room was all she could think about, yet she applied restraint for the time being. It became another good decision; two more people could now be seen walking toward her. Yasti quickly started rummaging through the cleaning cart to continue her ruse as a maid. She occasionally risked a brief glance up in order to identify the individuals getting closer with each step. Yasti became shocked! A large bunch of very red hair was moving her way. It could only belong to one person, Kaylee.

How did she end up here? questioned Yasti to herself.

In a split second, it became clear to Yasti that the rescue would be even more complicated than she previously considered. *And just what is behind this door?* she wondered.

Showdown

Raf woke up with information streaming across his mind. It seemed whenever he had a passing thought, that idea would grow exponentially. All he wanted to think about was the girl lying next to him in bed. So he bent all thoughts on her. Images of Shinar flashed in his mind. A Facebook profile picture showed up. Then some school pics were added. Her educational history came next. These weren't the kind of thoughts Raf was hoping for. He remembered the chip!

It must be turned on, he thought. *Mammon*, he spoke silently inside his mind.

Raf tested it out; he focused on Purgatory this time. Instantly, images of newspaper articles were visible to his mind. Internet commentaries about the City in Space followed.

He tried to turn off the chip again. *Mammon off.* He waited a moment. His next focus was on Dubai. Without hesitation, a view of the city was displayed in his head. The Burj Khalifa came after. *This was going to take some getting used to*, he thought. Obviously, there was no turning off parts of the chip. Raf began wondering if he wanted such a thing connected to his brain.

Suddenly, an overwhelming feeling shot through his entire body. He now had something to compare it to. It was somewhat like the new sensation he had just experienced the previous night during the physical connection with Shinar. Once again, unbeknownst to Raf, the chip released another dose of dopamine. Any negative emotions related to the chip were dispelled. Raf embraced the side effects of the microchip as a manageable attribute he could deal with. In fact, he took it a step further and decided to share his newfound ability with his favorite person.

"Good morning, Shinar." Even at low volume Raf's extraordinarily strong voice resonated across the hotel room.

Shinar embraced the vibrations that emanated from Raf's vocal cords. When he spoke, it was like a pleasurable shockwave that went deep into her bones. She reluctantly opened her eyes to grab Raf's unclothed arm and wrap it around her naked body.

A soft feminine voice was uttered. "Good morning, my love." Her words cut straight to his emotions.

Raf responded by pulling Shinar into himself. "Ask me a question."

Without pausing, she did as he requested. "Do you love me?"

He was taken aback for a second. This question could not be quantified by himself or the chip. No images were shown to his mind. He mustered a response. "Yes, more than anything else."

Shinar kissed his large hand.

Raf now asked her for a question related to something more tangible and difficult to answer.

She took a moment to think, then tried to stump him. "Okay, how far away is the Dark Planet from here?"

The instant that query entered Raf's ears, the answer appeared. He recited it back to Shinar, "If you mean TrES-2b, the distance from this earth in miles is 4,410 trillion."

"What!" was all she could say.

He continued, "The planet is identified as the darkest known exoplanet. Its gaseous composition puts it in the category of 'hot Jupiters.'"

Shinar suspected it was the microchip in Raf's head that enabled his newfound intelligence. Reen had made her aware of its capabilities some time before it was presented to Raf.

She embraced the dynamic edge it was beginning to apply to her special man.

"That's awesome, honey. How do you feel?"

"Smarter," replied Raf.

They both chuckled a little.

*****

Yasti knew she would have to open that door and probably very soon. She rummaged through her array of weapons to choose what she deemed would fit into her newly formed plan. Yasti wasn't intent on randomly killing people. Before leaving Purgatory, she'd asked Palmer to adjust one of the weapons she wanted to take with her to earth. The brain freeze device was dialed down a bit. Neither Palmer nor Yasti had actually tried it on a person yet, though she was willing to now. The disruptor weapons had no need to be modified; their severity was regulated by the user.

Yasti initiated her plan by slowly trying the knob on the door. As anticipated, it was locked and didn't turn. She grabbed the ring of keys and very quietly attempted to find the right one. When the correct key unlocked the door, Yasti invited the Spirit to enter the fray with her as she penetrated the unfamiliar room. She wrapped a towel over her left hand to conceal a brain freeze. Two disruptors were resting in their holsters under her loose-fitting garments.

Yasti slowly opened the door while moving the cart in front of herself. A nonchalant manner was her ploy. As far as everyone in the room was concerned, she was there to clean, though she didn't expect to be received well. What she saw next amazed her. Most of the traveling party was there. Many guards, all sporting guns, immediately noticed her; some even pointed their weapons at her. Yasti humbly inched toward the small crowd. Resnik's eyes connected with hers. They instantly developed an understanding between one another.

There were two men in the room dressed in a professional manner. One of them barked out a command, "Hey, we don't need any cleaning now! Turn around and go somewhere else."

Yasti feigned as if she didn't know English. A couple of armed men approached her. When they got close enough to grab her, she reached out and touched them with the brain freeze. They dropped as the showdown began. She squatted down behind her cart and drew out the two single-handed disruptors. She fired, and two more guards went down. Resnik, Gettie, and Neko went to work. Most of the guards hesitated for a nanosecond, not knowing where to direct their attention. Neko used the electronic notepad to smash Qusay's face. She followed by putting all her strength into a straightforward kick to his solar plexus. He went backward; she followed him as he hit the floor. For good measure, Neko grabbed fistfuls of thick black hair and thrust Qusay's head to the tile. His eyes closed.

Gettie also didn't hesitate to act. He had been watching the large guard hold Kaylee's slender arm with a vice-like grip. It took all his effort to hold back attacking the large man, until now. Gettie lunged forward with great momentum to slam his open hand to the chest of the guard holding Kaylee. The large man released his grip and fell back, out of breath. Gettie delivered a roundhouse punch to the guard's head. Then another and another until the man crumpled to the floor.

Yasti kept firing on the armed guards. She had them pinned behind a desk. She hadn't used a disruptor on an inanimate object before. She decided to try. One blast to the desk resulted in a loud bang. The desk moved back several feet along with two surprised security guards. Yasti liked it! Both disruptors were now raised; she fired simultaneously. The weakened desk blew apart, sending the men backward until they hit a wall. They were out cold. While that commotion was going on, Resnik was busy disarming the last two conscious guards. Yasti moved in quickly with the Syn-app to finish them off.

No one took the time to notice a small man squatting down to avoid being in the crossfire. A. L. Sek stood up brandishing a gun dropped by one of the guards. He pointed it directly at Kaylee's heart.

"Experiment over," he said audibly, though he was basically talking to himself. Without hesitating, he squeezed the trigger. Blood spattered against those closest to Kaylee. Shock filled the hearts of all those still standing in the room. A. L. Sek immediately turned the weapon on Resnik, his number one enemy. An empty click was heard. He had used the last round on his one-time daughter. To everyone in the room, the sound was as loud as a car crash. In the brief moments of confusion, all attention was diverted to Kaylee. A. L. Sek realized he had one last opportunity to inflict damage on Resnik. With an intent to move faster than he had ever done before, A. L. Sek stepped toward Resnik and used the butt end of the rifle to knock him out. Resnik went down.

Adrenaline was still pulsing through Neko's muscles. She locked her fingers together to create one large fist. She built up momentum by spinning her slender body in a 360-degree motion to slam her hands into Sek's head. An enormous thud resonated across the room. Sek and the rifle hit the floor hard.

All attention now turned to Kaylee. Gettie was holding her on his lap, his left hand was attempting to block the flow of blood from her neck. It seemed Sek's aim had missed Kaylee's heart and severed her left carotid artery.

"You're my beautiful boy," she said in a whispered tone as she gazed upward at Gettie.

He had just gotten her back. He refused to lose her again. Gettie risked a quick glance to see if his father was conscious and able to help. His mother was holding Resnik as Gettie was holding Kaylee. There was nothing else—nor anyone else—to help his beloved wife. He needed something preternatural.

"I'm getting cold, honey." Kaylee's words were barely audible.

Gettie blocked out all thoughts and emotions in his mind except those of the young woman on his lap. He invited the Spirit into his situation, then concentrated with all his heart to heal Kaylee. He'd seen his dad heal people, though he never really thought he possessed the gift himself. Now he dug deep to find out. He placed his free hand on Kaylee's heart, which was slowing down. He connected with the Spirit, uttering imperceptible words.

He could now no longer feel her heart; it had stopped beating. Discouragement was beckoning to him. He refused to be pulled into it. He kept faith in what he was doing. His focus did not lapse. He could feel warmth returning to his left hand. He looked down; no more of Kaylee's blood was spilling onto it. Instead, he could feel a pulse from her artery.

Her chest started rising and falling in rhythm. Gettie's tears were hitting her forehead. Neko and Yasti's eyes were also welling up.

Suddenly steps could be heard running down the hall. This pathetic group was hardly in a position to engage more opposition. Though Yasti could always be counted on to be battle ready. She bent down to one knee with a disruptor in each hand, facing the door. Footsteps were getting louder, and closer. Suddenly they stopped, the door swung open with force. An unarmed man was breathing hard; he paused to catch his wind.

After a few seconds, he spoke: "I've been waiting for you."

Yasti stayed her weapons. Neko instantly recognized him—William Parti! Only Resnik and Neko will have remembered the one-time betrayer, though Gettie glanced up and recognized William from the weathered photo in the tree.

"I can get you out safely, if we hurry!" he said with urgency.

That statement seemed unlikely. Resnik was still unconscious, and Kaylee seemed to be sleeping peacefully.

Yasti looked at Neko, She gave her a nod of approval. Yasti holstered her weapons and pulled out a communication device from inside her garb. She connected with Palmer; "There's a guy here who said he can help us get out of harm. Can you get us off-planet?" Yasti felt Palmer was the most qualified pilot in an emergency situation.

William overheard the request. "I can get you out, but I can't secure the landing pad. Epygen's people are watching for *Ornan*."

Palmer overheard William. "I might be able to manage."

Yasti was quickly taken aback to her last conversation with Palmer when he stated the need to recharge *Ornan* at the landing pad. She was mentally stuck. She once again looked toward Neko.

"Try it!" said Neko. She had given Palmer some insight into energy before her trip to Earth. Along with Guardian tech, she was hoping he could find a way to recharge *Ornan* without the need from outside sources; now may be the time to test it out.

"Come immediately" was Yasti's directive to Palmer. "Can you bring Leal? Two of our group are injured."

Once again, William dispensed with courteous protocol. Time was short. He blurted out, "I can help. I'd like to go with all of you!"

Everyone paused, that was a substantial request. "Bring him!" stated a groggy voice. Resnik had gotten everyone's attention. He slowly opened his eyes and connected with Neko. He didn't have to say anything else. Neko then gave another nod to Yasti.

"Forget about Leal. Just come quick," was Yasti's last request to Palmer.

Ninety minutes was a long time to wait. First, they had to get out of Epygen with two injured members of the landing party. Resnik began the process of getting to his feet; he understood the urgency of the situation.

Gettie was unsure if he should wake Kaylee.

"I don't know if we should move her," he questioned out loud.

"I can go, with your help," Kaylee's voice was noticeably stronger.

"I'll carry you if I have to," was his response.

They all followed William through a secret passageway. It was slow going, and the tunnel passageway was long. The exit emerged under and across the street in front of Epygen. In their haste, they left without knowing who among the casualties of the showdown were alive or dead.

Once free of Epygen, the group of six attempted to get to a clearing of some kind. William was very helpful in this endeavor; he knew the neighborhood. It would take a bit more walking but they were still ahead of *Ornan*'s landing. Yasti took the opportunity to pull out her Earth cell phone and call Raf. An obviously sleepy Raf answered the call. The time was eleven hours different in that part of the world.

He agreed to meet them outside the city in the open desert— that was if *Ornan* was up to the challenge.

Palmer knew how to track Yasti; he could find her as long as she carried at least one of the electronic devices. In fact, he was already adjusting his trajectory to pinpoint her location as the six of them slowly walked to an open area. Enough time had gone by to cause Yasti to periodically look up to see if the triangle shape of *Ornan* was getting close. It had been every bit of ninety minutes as Palmer touched down in a parking lot on planet Earth in very close proximity to Yasti and the others.

"Good to see you, son," were Resnik's first words to Palmer upon landing. "Are we going to be able to take off again?"

"I hope so, sir," Palmer was busy helping everyone board the ship. He then singled out Neko. He became anxious to show her a perfect- looking container made out of a metal alloy. It was pill-shaped, about the size of a small football. It certainly mimicked other containers received from a Guardian. "They're in here," he said with a slight grin on his face.

Neko had captured several boson particles during her last stay on Purgatory, and now they resided within this flawless container. Her big eyes were cautiously optimistic as they peered at the star tech.

"Let's try it." He inserted the boson-rich container into a special area of *Ornan*. Nothing happened! Everyone on board became extremely nervous. A quick glimpse around showed curious people entering the parking lot, cell phones in hand.

Neko now wore a determined look on her face as she spoke up, "It's okay. *Ornan*'s drive engine is negotiating with this new form of energy. Give it a moment. It's learning."

Sure enough, gauges started displaying information, the yoke moved into position, and subtle interior lights came on. Palmer was now ready to input the coordinates to their next destination. "United Arab Emirates, right?" asked Palmer?

Yasti responded, "That's correct."

Resnik put his arm around Neko, "You're amazing, honey."

This was *Ornan*'s first time going from one Earth destination to another. Palmer wasn't even sure at what altitude he wanted to fly from California to Dubai. He winged it.

*****

Shinar drove Raf in her car to the open desert. On the way, she expressed a concern, "I don't want to be without you."

It was automatic for Raf to just go back to the City in Space. He felt like the power of the chip would allow him to talk to Shinar from Purgatory, but maybe she was right. Why should he go back to space? His real family resides on Earth. Of course, his mother was surely waiting for him on Purgatory. Could she really be trusted? She certainly delayed telling him about his heritage.

Shinar broke the silence, "We love you here, you have a very promising future on Earth. The Prophet is counting on you."

After all, he actually had a choice. And he really couldn't leave Shinar now. He was in love. They could see sand flying everywhere as *Ornan* was coming in for a landing. Raf quickly realized he was certainly going to get some pushback from those on board if he stayed. A showdown was imminent.

Shinar and Raf waited for the sand to settle before driving close to *Ornan*. Raf's resolve was finalized in his mind now. He got out of the car with Shinar in tow.

As soon as Resnik stepped out of the ship, he was able to read Raf's demeanor. He became very concerned for Raf. Resnik put his hand out to greet him.

"Hello, son. Are you ready to go home?" Resnik could feel a somewhat darkened change within Raf through the handshake.

"I am home, sir."

Resnik now put his hand out to Shinar. She took it in kind. "I'm Resnik Clayborn. Nice to meet you." She leaned into Raf while offering her hand to Resnik, "I'm Shinar."

Just then, Gettie came out of *Ornan* running to embrace Raf. "Let's go, you big lug, what are you waiting for?"

"I'm staying here," was his response.

Gettie had a surprised look on his face. He went further, "You don't know anyone here, where will you live?" He asked these questions but had a pretty good idea Raf was planning on staying with the girl holding his hand.

"There are many others like me here," answered Raf.

"Like you?" asked Gettie.

"Yes, descendants of the Nephilim. They're my real family."

Gettie became instantly saddened. "But we're brothers."

Shinar put her free hand on Raf's arm. He pushed on, "They're my aunts, uncles, and cousins. Many of them look like me. And they want me to lead their new organization."

Gettie couldn't believe what he was hearing, "And just what is that?"

"The New World Order."

Automobiles were already driving to see the vessel that stirred up so much sand in the open desert. Resnik grabbed Gettie's arm, "We've got to go!"

Raf offered a last statement. "G-goodbye, b-brother, I…I'm sta- staying ha-here."

www.ingramcontent.com/pod-product-compliance
Lightning Source LLC
Chambersburg PA
CBHW022051050726
47591CB00002B/492